E.B

"I can sti

Yeah, so could he. He didn't want to tell her that she would hear them for the rest of her life. But she would. So would he. And he would remember that look of terror on her face.

There wasn't really a way to comfort her right now so Drury just slipped his arm around her and hoped that helped. It seemed to do that. For a couple of long moments anyway. Until she lifted her head, and her eyes met his.

Any chance of comforting her vanished. A lot of things vanished. Like common sense, because just like that, Drury felt the old attraction.

"I don't know how to stop this," she said. Her voice was a whisper, filled with her thin breath.

She wasn't talking about the danger now.

It would have been safer if she had been.

Before he could talk himself out of it or remember this was something he shouldn't be doing, Drury lowered his head and kissed her.

DRURY

USA TODAY Bestselling Author

DELORES FOSSEN

Recycling programs
for this product may
not exist in your area.

ISBN-13: 978-0-373-75667-4

Drury

Delores Fossen, a *USA TODAY* bestselling author, has sold over fifty novels with millions of copies of her books in print worldwide. She's received a Booksellers' Best Award and an RT Reviewers' Choice Best Book Award. She was also a finalist for a prestigious RITA® Award. You can contact the author through her website at www.deloresfossen.com.

Books by Delores Fossen

Harlequin Intrigue

The Lawmen of Silver Creek Ranch

Grayson
Dade
Nate
Kade
Gage
Mason
Josh
Sawyer
Landon
Holden
Drury

HQN Books

A Wrangler's Creek Novel

Lone Star Cowboy (ebook novella)
Those Texas Nights
One Good Cowboy (ebook novella)
No Getting Over a Cowboy

Visit the Author Profile page at Harlequin.com for more titles.

CAST OF CHARACTERS

FBI agent Drury Ryland—He thought he'd gotten over his ex, Caitlyn Denson, until she shows up at the Silver Creek Ranch with a baby and a killer after her. Drury knows the child isn't his, but that won't stop him from doing his job and protecting them.

Caitlyn Denson—Years ago she walked out on Drury because she couldn't cope with his dangerous career, but now Drury is the one man who can save her and a newborn who might be her own daughter—a daughter Caitlyn didn't even know existed until after the child was born.

The baby—This newborn girl was born because someone stole an embryo from a fertility clinic, but who are her biological parents?

Grant Denson—Caitlyn's late husband, who was killed in a car accident nearly two years ago. When they were trying to have a child, they did use a fertility clinic, so it's possible the stolen embryo is theirs.

Melanie Cordova—She's Grant's former mistress. She hates Caitlyn, but does that hatred extend to a child who might be Caitlyn and Grant's?

Jeremy Denson—Grant's younger brother. He claims the last thing he wants is a Denson heir who could be his competition to inherit the vast family estate.

Helen Denson—The matriarch of the Denson family. She's bitter about having lost her son and would perhaps do anything to make sure a part of him has lived on.

Chapter One

Special Agent Drury Ryland pulled into his driveway, his truck headlights slashing through the curtain of rain. Rain that nearly caused him to miss the movement behind his detached garage.

Nearly.

But Drury managed to catch a glimpse of someone darting out of sight.

He groaned because it wasn't exactly the hour or the weather for a visitor. Or the place. He was home, in one of the nearly dozen houses on the sprawling Silver Creek Ranch, and all those houses were occupied by lawmen. Anyone who'd come here to break in was a couple of steps past being stupid.

Of course, it might not be a break-in.

Because Drury's arm was still throbbing from the six stitches he had just gotten, he had no trouble recalling the encounter he'd had three hours earlier. A thug had knifed him during an FBI sting operation. Drury had managed to arrest him, but the guy had sworn on his soul that he would get even with Drury. No way could the soul-swearing guy have gotten out of jail yet, but he could have sent one of his buddies to do his dirty work.

Drury brought his truck to a stop, eased his hand over his gun and tried to pick through the darkness and rain so he could get another glimpse of the guy. Nothing. But Drury knew he was there.

"I'm Agent Drury Ryland," he shouted. "Come out so I can see you."

The guy didn't. And not only didn't he come out, he fired a shot. Before Drury could even react, the bullet slammed into his windshield.

The next two shots went straight into his truck's engine. One must have hit the radiator because steam started spewing into the air.

Drury cursed. There went his way to escape. If he wanted to escape, that is. He didn't. He wanted to confront this moron and make him pay for starting a gunfight on Ryland land.

Since the sound of the shots would no doubt alert his cousins and brothers, Drury sent a quick text to one of those cousins, Sheriff Grayson Ryland, and requested backup. However, Drury was hoping he could put an end to the situation before backup even arrived.

Drury threw open his truck door, and using

it for cover, he took aim at the shadowy figure that kept peering around the garage. He couldn't just start pulling the trigger, though. It had to be a clean shot because Drury didn't want it to ricochet and risk hitting a ranch hand or someone inside one of the nearby houses.

The shooter obviously didn't have that concern because he fired off another round at Drury. Big mistake. Because he had to lean out from the garage, and Drury took the shot.

And hit the guy.

Not a kill shot, though. He must have hit him in the shoulder because the gunman took off running. A few seconds later, Drury heard the sound of an engine.

No.

He didn't want this clown getting away. Drury had to find out why the heck he'd just tried to kill him.

A dark-colored SUV sped out from behind the garage. Not coming toward Drury. But rather the driver went on the other side of the house, through the yard and onto the road. Since there weren't any houses at this angle, Drury emptied the clip into the SUV.

Drury was certain he hit the guy again, but he kept going, speeding away from the house. He was about to jump in his truck and try to go in pursuit, but then Drury saw Grayson's cruiser approaching. Grayson was not only the sheriff of Silver Creek, but he lived the closest and that's why Drury had texted him.

When Grayson reached Drury, he put down the window, and Drury saw he wasn't alone. Grayson's brother Mason was with him.

"Any idea who's in that SUV?" Grayson asked.

Drury had to shake his head, but he lifted his arm to show them the fresh bandage. "Maybe a friend of the person who gave me this."

"We'll go after him," Grayson said. "Keep watch. Make sure he doesn't double back."

Since Drury's place was the first house on the road that led to the ranch, that wouldn't be hard to do.

When Grayson drove off in pursuit, Drury had a look around the grounds. He didn't see anyone else, though. And if his attacker had left any blood by the garage, the rain was washing it all away. That made it even more critical for Grayson to find him so Drury could get some answers.

He went to his back porch and cursed when he found the door unlocked. It was possible he'd just forgotten to lock it. Just as possible, though, that someone had broken in.

Especially after what'd just happened.

Drury got his gun ready and kicked open the door that led into his kitchen.

"Don't shoot," someone said.

A woman.

Because she'd whispered that order, Drury didn't immediately recognize her voice, but he certainly knew who she was when she stepped closer.

Caitlyn Denson.

The kitchen was dark, but there was enough illumination coming from the hall light that he had no trouble seeing her long brown hair and her face.

And the blood trickling down her forehead.

Drury didn't know what shocked him the most. The blood or that she was even there at all. They weren't exactly on friendly terms and hadn't been in a long time.

He had so many questions, and he wasn't sure where to start. But his lawman's instincts kicked in, and he checked her hands for weapons. Empty. And the pale yellow dress she was wearing was wet and clinging to her, so he knew she wasn't carrying concealed.

Still, he didn't lower his gun. He kept it aimed at her. And he maneuvered himself so he could watch out the large bay window in the living room while still keeping an eye on Caitlyn.

"I heard you'd built a house here on your cousins' ranch, and your name is on the mailbox. I parked behind your barn," she said, as if that explained everything.

It didn't, not by a long shot.

"Did you have anything to do with that?" Drury tipped his head to the side yard where the shots had just been fired.

Caitlyn's eyes widened for just a second, and a thin breath left her mouth. "I think he was here because he's looking for me. I swear, I didn't know he'd follow me."

Well, it was an answer all right. But it only led to more questions. "You're going to have to give me a better explanation than that. And start with how you got that cut or whatever the hell it is." He grabbed some paper towels with his left hand and gave them to her.

She nodded and pressed the towels to her head. "I didn't break in, by the way. The door was unlocked, but you should know that I would have broken in if necessary. I needed a place to hide." She staggered, caught the back of the chair.

Drury cursed and went to her, holstering his gun so he could help her get seated and have a look at the wound that was causing her to bleed all over his kitchen floor. His stomach knotted when he saw the wound close-up.

"Did someone club you on the head?" he asked.

Caitlyn nodded, lightly touched the wound and grimaced when she saw the blood on her fingertips. "I'm not certain who did it. I didn't get a look at his face. But it could have been the same man who shot at you."

And if so, the thug had come to finish what he'd started, and Drury had gotten caught in the middle. Caught only because she'd come here. But why?

"You're sure you don't know who he is?" Drury pressed.

Even though he didn't spell it out, she obviously got what he meant. Was this connected to her late husband, Grant Denson? Grant had been dead for nearly two years now, but he'd been involved in some nasty illegal stuff when he was alive that might now have come back to haunt Caitlyn.

Of course, when you sleep with snakes, you should expect to get bitten.

Was that what had happened now?

"I honestly don't know the man's name," she explained. "But I know why he's after me." Her voice broke, and a hoarse sob tore from her mouth. "God, Drury, I'm so sorry. I didn't have anywhere else to go, and I didn't think he'd come here."

All right. That got his interest. Because she had a mother-in-law, Helen, who was loaded, not just money-wise but with all sorts of resources, including but not limited to thugs who could take care of the person who'd clubbed Caitlyn on the head.

"Start from the beginning," he demanded.

Caitlyn didn't exactly jump to do that, but she

did nod again and then took a couple of seconds to gather her breath. "The year before Grant was killed, we were trying to have a baby, and we went to the Conceptions Fertility Clinic in San Antonio."

Everything inside him went still. He was well aware of the clinic because of the shady things that'd happened there just a month earlier. Specifically, embryos had been stolen and implanted in surrogates so that the former clinic manager could then "sell" the babies to the biological parents.

Ransom, extortion and black-market babies all rolled into one. Nasty business.

"All the babies were recovered and given to their parents," Drury reminded her.

Caitlyn paused a heartbeat. "Not all."

"Are you saying…?" But he stopped. "What the hell are you saying?"

"Day before yesterday I got a call from a man who said a surrogate had given birth to mine and Grant's daughter and that if I wanted the child, then I'd have to pay him a million dollars. He sent me a swab with the baby's DNA, and I had it analyzed. The man was telling the truth."

DNA could be faked. So could test results.

"And?" Drury questioned. "How did you get Grant's DNA to do a comparison?"

"From a comb I found in his things that I'd boxed up."

Drury made a circling motion for her to continue.

"I arranged payment, draining nearly every penny from Grant's estate, but when I went to get the baby, she wasn't there. Instead, the man demanded even more money."

Drury groaned. "Let me guess. They told you not to go to the cops or that you'd never see her again?" He waited for her to confirm that with a nod. "That's what criminals tell marks like you. Hell, they might not even have the baby. Or there might not be a baby at all. Even if the DNA appears to prove it's your child, they could have gotten the DNA from an embryo sample stored at the clinic."

Other than a soft moan, she didn't get a chance to respond because Drury's phone rang. "It's Grayson," he said, glancing at the screen.

That got her back on her feet, and Caitlyn shook her head. "Please don't tell him I'm here. Not yet. I'm not sure who I can trust."

"Well, you can't trust me," he snapped.

But that was a lie. He was a lawman and would do whatever it took to protect her or any other bleeding woman who showed up at his house.

"Please," she repeated, sounding just as desperate as she looked.

Drury wasn't going to let that *please* or desperation sway him. He intended to tell Grayson everything because while she might not trust his cousin, Drury darn sure did.

"We found the shooter," Grayson said the moment Drury answered the call. "He'd crashed his SUV into a tree about three miles from the ranch. He's hurt but alive."

"Who is he?" Drury asked.

"No ID, and the vehicle is registered to a woman in Austin."

Maybe that meant the SUV was stolen. Of course, Drury already knew this guy was a criminal capable of murder. "Did he happen to say why he fired shots at me or what he was doing at my place?" Drury pressed.

Caitlyn moved closer. Too close. No doubt trying to hear the conversation.

"He's not saying much of anything. He's groggy, slipping in and out of consciousness," Grayson added. "We'll get him to the hospital, but I did find something in the SUV that was, well, disturbing. Some rope, a ski mask, duct tape and rubber gloves."

No baby. Though Drury hadn't expected there would be. Caitlyn had likely been the victim of a scam, and now that they couldn't milk any more money from her, this thug had been sent to get rid of her.

"I'll head to the sheriff's office now," Drury insisted.

"You need a ride? When I drove by earlier, I saw your truck was messed up."

"Yeah. That thug shot the radiator. But I have a car in the garage. I'll also have someone with me who can shed some light on this."

Caitlyn was shaking her head before he even finished.

"Who?" Grayson asked, but he continued before Drury could respond. "Gotta go. Ambulance is here. You can tell me when you get to the office. See you in a few."

"No," Caitlyn said, still shaking her head when Drury ended the call. "You shouldn't have done that. You shouldn't have told Grayson you were bringing someone in."

And she took off. Not toward the door but rather into the living room.

"What the heck do you think you're doing?" Drury asked.

She didn't answer that. Caitlyn hurried to the side of the sofa, and she grabbed something from the floor. Even though the room was dark, Drury had no trouble seeing the bundled-up coat.

And the stun gun.

Caitlyn picked up both, and with the coat clutched to her chest, she started running, headed to the back door this time.

Drury stepped in front of her, blocking her path, but Caitlyn tried to dart around him. He didn't want her to get a chance to use that stun gun on him, so he caught onto her arm and knocked the stun gun from her hand.

"I have to go," she insisted. "It's not safe."

Maybe it wasn't, but that didn't mean Drury was just going to let her head out. He pulled her closer and had a better look at the coat.

Damn.

In the middle of that bundle, Drury saw something move.

And that something was a baby.

Chapter Two

Caitlyn hadn't expected Drury just to let her walk out of there, but she also hadn't thought this insanity would go from bad to worse.

This definitely qualified as worse.

Now that he'd seen the baby, there was no way he'd willingly let her leave.

"The baby's yours?" he snapped.

"Maybe."

She'd figured Drury wasn't going to like that answer, and he didn't. He groaned. Then cursed.

"But I believe she's mine," Caitlyn went on. "And the man said she was. I figured I could have her tested later, but for now I have to go. That man who shot at you wants to kill me and take the baby."

"Yeah. I got that. According to Grayson, he had rope, tape, a ski mask and gloves in his SUV. All the makings of a felony or two."

Oh, God. Her stomach dropped. Even though

Caitlyn had known the man didn't have good intentions, it sickened her to hear it spelled out like that. It also confirmed what she'd felt in her heart.

That he had no intention of giving her the baby.

He'd had plans to kill her then and there. She doubted he had just stopped trying to do that, either.

"The man will send someone else after me," Caitlyn tried again. Tried also to move past Drury, but, like before, he stopped her.

Mercy, she had to convince him to let her go. But how? Too bad her head was throbbing and she was dizzy because it made it hard to think.

"Look, I know you don't owe me any favors," she said. "But let me leave."

An understatement about the favors.

And the sound Drury made let her know that he didn't owe her a thing. Not after she'd walked out on him four years ago. He'd been in love with her. *Then.* Definitely not now, though. There wasn't a shred of love between them at this moment.

However, Caitlyn could still feel the tug of attraction. The one she'd had for Drury the first time she'd laid eyes on him. That attraction was all one-sided now, on her part. Drury's glare proved it.

"Please just help me by letting me leave right now," she begged.

It seemed to take him a couple of seconds to

get his jaw unclenched so he could speak, and he didn't look at her when he did it. He volleyed his attention between the baby and the window. Drury was no doubt looking to see if the thug had indeed sent someone else to come after her.

Good.

Because Caitlyn was looking, too.

"How'd you get the baby?" Drury asked.

She huffed. There wasn't time for all this talk, but it was obvious he wasn't going to let her leave until he had some answers. Maybe not even then. That meant she had to get away at the first chance she got.

"I took her from that man," Caitlyn said, blinking back the tears that were burning her eyes. Her voice, like the rest of her, was trembling. "I really don't know who he is, and I didn't see his face. He was wearing a ski mask."

"Keep talking," Drury insisted when she paused again.

"I was meeting him to deliver another payment, but this time I brought a stun gun with me."

Mercy. It was hard to relive this. The memories were still so fresh and raw. The fear, too.

"When I handed him the money," she went on, "I reached for the baby. He smashed me on the head with his weapon, but I was able to hit him with the stun gun. He fell to the ground. I grabbed the baby and got away."

No groan this time. Drury cursed again instead. "You could have been killed."

"I could have lost her," Caitlyn pointed out just as quickly. "Even if she's not my daughter, she belongs to someone, and I had to get her away from that monster."

Drury didn't seem swayed in the least by that. "You should have involved the cops."

"I couldn't because the man said he'd know if I brought anyone with me." In addition to the tears and trembling, Caitlyn had to fight the sudden tightness in her chest. "He said he would hurt the baby if I wasn't alone. I couldn't risk it."

She must have looked ready to fly into a million little pieces because Drury huffed. Then did something surprising. He touched her arm. It barely qualified as a pat, but she'd take it.

Too bad he didn't offer her a hug, or she would have taken that, too.

The touch didn't last long. Drury looked at her, his gaze lingering for a moment before it also slipped away.

"During any of your conversations, did this clown say if he was working for someone or how he got the baby in the first place?" Drury asked.

"No. But I'm not sure he's connected to anyone at Conceptions Clinic." She hesitated about adding the next part. Not because it wasn't true.

It was.

But it wasn't going to shorten this conversation. "I think the man might be working for Helen Denson."

There, she'd said it aloud. Her worst fear. Or rather, one of them. She had plenty of others at the moment, but at the top of that list was that her dead husband's rich, manipulative mother could be the one who'd orchestrated this nightmare.

Caitlyn could almost see the wheels turning in Drury's head, and he was likely trying to work out why she'd just accused her former mother-in-law of such a heinous crime.

"Helen hates me," Caitlyn explained. "And she was furious when she found out Grant left his entire estate to me. I think she would do anything, including something like this, to get back the money."

Of course, that could mean the baby wasn't hers. After all, Helen could have used any baby to carry out a scheme like that.

"Why would Helen be upset about you inheriting what belonged to your husband?" he asked.

This was another long explanation, one she didn't have time or energy to give him. Caitlyn went with the short version. "Grant and I were separated when he was killed in that car accident. I was already in the process of getting a divorce."

He pulled back his shoulders just slightly. Surprised by that. Later, if there was a later, she would tell him more. For now, though, she had to remind him of the urgency of her situation.

"That man who had the baby wasn't working alone," she continued. "When I made the first payment, there were two of them, and I'm pretty sure they had a lookout or someone nearby because one of the men had a communicator in his ear, and he was talking to someone. I can't stay here because they'll come back."

"Come on," Drury said. He still had a firm grip on her arm. "We'll go to the sheriff's office and get this all straightened out."

"They'll look for me there if they don't attack us along the way first. The baby could be hurt. You, too." She almost added that she couldn't live with that, but it was an old wound best left untouched.

"If you didn't want me involved, then you shouldn't have come here," he grumbled.

"I swear I didn't know the man would follow me. I mean, he was out from the stun gun, and he didn't have his partner with him this time. Didn't have the communicator in his ear, either." A heavy sigh left her mouth. "I guess he had a lookout after all."

Caitlyn figured Drury would ignore everything she'd just told him and demand once more that she leave with him.

But he didn't.

His gaze volleyed from her to the baby. "Whose coat is that?" he asked.

She had to shake her head. "It was right next to the baby on the seat of the kidnapper's SUV, and I grabbed it to cover her from the rain."

"Put the baby on the sofa," Drury instructed, and his tone and body language sent a chill straight through her. "It could have a tracking device—or something worse—in it."

Sweet heaven.

Caitlyn hurried to the sofa, easing the baby onto it. The little girl was still sleeping, thank goodness.

"I checked her after I brought her into your house," she explained. "No cuts or bruises." It sickened her, though, to think there could have been.

Drury didn't respond. He moved in front of the newborn, eased back the sides of the coat.

The baby was wearing a pink drawstring gown with little ducks on it. There was even an elastic headband with a bow holding back her dark brown curls from her face, and she had a thin receiving blanket around her. She was clean. Her diaper appeared to have been changed recently, and since she wasn't crying, that probably meant she'd been fed. Whoever had her had at least taken care of her.

Probably so they could protect their *investment*.

Something twisted inside Caitlyn at the thought.

She almost hated to feel this kind of anger. This kind of love for that precious little girl. Because the baby might not even be hers.

Caitlyn repeated that to herself.

It didn't seem to stop the flood of feelings that poured through her, and that love could mean she would be crushed if she had to hand over the baby to someone else.

"Lift her up," Drury said, still searching every inch of the coat. "Gently."

That gave her another jolt, and she prayed there wasn't anything on or near the baby that could hurt her.

Caitlyn eased the newborn into her arms. Of course, it wasn't the first time she'd held her, but without the coat around her, she could feel just how tiny and fragile she was.

Drury went through the coat pockets, coming up empty each time, and he turned his attention to the bow on the baby's headband.

"Hell," he mumbled.

Caitlyn watched as he gently slipped off the headband, and she saw it then.

"It's a tracking device," he said. "That's how the man was able to follow you."

Caitlyn shook her head. "I should have noticed it. Drury. I'm so sorry."

"Save it." He tossed the headband onto the coffee table. "In case I missed something, don't use the blanket to wrap her." He pulled a throw off the back of the sofa and handed it to her. "Use this."

"Where are we going?" she asked, draping it over the baby.

"Away from here. And fast." He took out his phone and sent a text. Probably to Grayson. "I don't want any other hired guns coming to the ranch. Every one of my cousins has wives and kids, and they're all right here on the grounds."

That didn't help steady her heartbeat.

Drury led her to the back door, grabbing a remote control from the kitchen counter. He used it to open the detached garage, and he stepped out onto the porch to look around.

The rain was still coming down hard, but the porch was covered so the baby was staying dry. However, she was starting to squirm, maybe because Caitlyn's dress was damp and it was cool against her. She needed dry clothes. Baby supplies.

And a safe place to take her.

But where?

The sheriff's office certainly didn't seem like an ideal location since the man's partners could go looking for her there.

"Wait here in the doorway, and I'll pull the car up to the steps," Drury said. He'd already started to walk away but then stopped and turned back around to face her. "So help me, you'd better not try to run."

Since she was indeed thinking just that, Caitlyn wondered if he'd read her mind. Or maybe he could just see the desperation on her face.

Because she didn't know what else to do, Caitlyn did wait. And she prayed. She trusted Drury, but her trust wouldn't do a darn thing to protect him or the baby.

He hurried to the garage, and it took only a few seconds before she heard the engine turn on. Only a few seconds more before he pulled the car to the steps with the passenger's side facing her.

The moment Drury threw open the door and frantically motioned for her to get in, she knew something was wrong.

"Someone's coming," Drury said.

Caitlyn saw the headlights then. There was a car on the road. And it was speeding right toward them.

Chapter Three

Drury cursed himself for not getting Caitlyn away from the house any sooner. But he'd delayed because he hadn't been sure what was going on.

Still wasn't sure.

But he couldn't wait around and find out if whoever was in that car had friendly intentions. Judging from the tracking device he'd found, his guess was no. No friendly intentions here. That vehicle was likely carrying more shooters who'd come after Caitlyn and the baby. And being inside the house wouldn't necessarily help them if these morons opened fire.

Caitlyn ran down the porch steps, and Drury reached across the seat to pull her inside. The moment she was in, he gunned the engine to get them the heck out of there.

"You're not going to drive toward that car, are you?" she asked. The fear was right back in her voice. Not that it'd completely gone away, but there was a triple dose of it now.

It was raining, they didn't have a car seat and bullets might start flying at any second.

"We're not going toward the car," he assured her, and he bolted out of the side of his yard and headed not for the highway, but toward the main house.

It was a risk, but there were no completely safe options here.

Drury tossed her his phone. "Text Grayson and tell him what's going on. And climb in the back with the baby. Get all the way down on the seat and stay there."

She gave a shaky nod, and with the baby cradled in her arms, Caitlyn scrambled into the back. Drury heard her typing the text, but he kept his attention on the other car. Even though he hadn't turned on his headlights, the driver of the vehicle must have seen him because he came after them.

Hell.

He had hoped the guy would just back off when he saw where Drury was headed. No such luck.

Drury drove toward the main house, but he certainly had no intentions of stopping. There was a security gate just ahead, and like everybody else on the ranch, he had the remote to open and close it. He started pushing the remote button the moment it came into view, and the metal gates dragged open.

It seemed to take an eternity.

And that car behind him just kept getting closer and closer.

"He's got a gun," Caitlyn said, and that's when Drury realized she'd lifted her head and was looking out the back window.

"Get back down," he warned her.

Yeah, the guy had a gun all right. Drury had no trouble spotting it because the passenger lowered his window and stuck out his hand, trying to take aim.

The moment the gates were open, Drury gunned the engine and flew through them, hitting the remote to close them.

It worked.

The gates closed before the shooter could get through. The driver hit his brakes, slamming into the gate, but the gates held.

Thank God.

Drury kept going, and he sped past the houses that dotted the ranch. He didn't dare stop because the gunman might have a long-range rifle in the car, and Drury didn't want to give the guy any reason to keep firing.

"Grayson says his brothers and the ranch hands have been alerted," Caitlyn relayed after getting a response to the text she'd sent.

Good. Though he doubted that gunman would get out of the car and go in pursuit on foot, it was better to be safe than sorry.

Especially since Drury was already sorry enough for this fiasco.

He stayed on the road that coiled around the pastures, and once he was past the exterior security lights, it was too dark for him to see. Drury had no choice but to turn on his headlights.

"Where are we going?" she asked.

Some place she wouldn't like. "The sheriff's office. And before you remind me that these goons can follow us there, they can follow us anywhere. At least if we're at the sheriff's office, the deputies and I can protect you, and it'll get these idiots away from my family.

"Don't say you're sorry," he added, his voice a little harsher than he'd intended.

Drury had caught a glimpse of her face in the mirror and could tell from the tears that she was about to apologize again. Well, it wouldn't help. Nothing would right now except getting her and that baby to safety.

His phone rang, the sound cutting through the other sounds of his heartbeat drumming in his ears and the wipers slashing at the rain.

"It's Grayson," Caitlyn said. She passed him the phone, but since Drury still had hold of his gun, he pushed the speaker button and dropped the phone on the seat next to him.

"Where are you?" Grayson asked. "And what the heck's going on?"

"I'm at the back of the ranch on one of the trails and about to come out on Miller's Hill. The car with the gunmen didn't get past the gate."

"No," Grayson agreed. "Gage had eyes on the car, and he said the driver turned around and sped off. He got the license plate numbers, but they're bogus. Gage and Dade went in pursuit."

Both men were Grayson's brothers. And his deputies.

"I'll take the back roads to get to the sheriff's office. I should be there in about twenty minutes." Drury paused. "Caitlyn Denson is with me."

Grayson paused, too, and then cursed. A rarity for him since he was the father of a five-year-old son and had cut way back on his bad language.

"Caitlyn?" Grayson repeated like the profanity he'd just used. "You're not involved with her again, are you?"

"No, not like that." And Drury couldn't say it fast enough.

"Good. Because the last time you hooked up with her…"

Grayson didn't finish that. Didn't need to finish it. Because Drury remembered it well enough without any reminders. Caitlyn had been a CPA in those days. A CPA who'd been helping Drury investigate the crime family that had employed her.

At least Drury had believed she was helping him.

However, he'd been wrong. Because Caitlyn had ended up marrying the very man whose family Drury had been investigating. But those were old memories, and he didn't have time for them now.

"So, why is Caitlyn with you?" Grayson pressed. "And are those gunmen after her?"

"They're after her." That was the easy question to answer. The first one, not so much. "There might be another baby from Conceptions Clinic."

He gave Grayson a moment for that to sink in.

"Caitlyn and Grant Denson's baby," Grayson concluded.

"Yeah. At least that's what a man told Caitlyn." Drury could still see her in the glimpses that he was making in the rearview mirror, and she was hanging on to every word. "According to her, a man demanded a ransom. She paid it, but he reneged."

Grayson mumbled some profanity. "Where's the baby now?"

"In the backseat of my car with Caitlyn. She was waiting inside my place when I got home." He figured it wouldn't take Grayson long to fill in the blanks.

And it didn't.

"Caitlyn came to you for help."

Drury settled for another *yeah* and didn't miss Grayson's disapproval about that. Well, Drury wasn't so happy about it, either.

"I don't know for sure, but the guy you caught is probably the same one who had the baby. He should have stun-gun marks on…" Drury looked back at her so she could provide that.

"The left side of his neck."

Grayson made what sounded to be a weary sigh. "I'll have the doc check for it. I got a name on the guy already. Ronnie Waite. He was in the system not because he had a record but because he used to be a prison guard."

Interesting. Drury would have bet his paycheck that the guy had a record. But then maybe whoever was behind this had made sure to use someone who was clean.

"Ronnie Waite," Drury repeated to Caitlyn. He turned onto another road and glanced around to make sure they weren't being followed. "Do you know him?"

Caitlyn repeated the name, then shook her head. "Is he in charge of this or just a lackey?"

"Don't know yet," Grayson answered. "How did Ronnie or anyone connected to this contact you?"

"Only one man contacted me," Caitlyn answered, "and he always called. I used the internet to do a reverse number lookup, but it wasn't listed."

Probably because the phone had been a burner or disposable prepaid cell. No way to trace that. But if Ronnie still had the phone on him, Grayson would have it checked.

"Does Caitlyn, or the baby, need to see a doctor?" Grayson asked.

"Yes," Drury said at the same moment that she answered.

"No. I mean, I want the baby checked out, but I'm fine. And I don't want to be in the hospital while Ronnie is still there."

"Caitlyn's not fine," Drury argued. "She might have a concussion. But I agree about not going to the hospital. She shouldn't be there until we're certain Ronnie can't get near her."

"I'll have a medic come to the office then." Grayson paused. "We'll get into all of this once you're here, but I'll need you to think of anyone who could have hired this man."

"Helen," Drury and Caitlyn said in unison.

"All right. I'll get your former mother-in-law here for a chat," Grayson agreed without hesitation. "I'll also see if there's any way to connect her to Ronnie."

"There has to be a surrogate out there, too,"

Caitlyn added. "I'm not sure how to find her, but she might be linked somehow to Ronnie."

"I can question Ronnie about that. And check for a Jane Doe DB who might have recently given birth."

DB as in *dead body.*

Caitlyn made a slight gasping sound. Probably because she'd just realized what Grayson was saying—that the surrogate could have been murdered after she gave birth. Whoever was behind this wouldn't have wanted to keep a surrogate alive unless, of course, the surrogate was in on the plan.

"I'll have Mason call the lead investigator who handled the Conceptions Clinic case," Grayson went on, "but if Helen's the one who did this, would she have had access to the embryo? In other words, could someone at the clinic have legally given it to her?"

"No. Not legally." Caitlyn drew in a long breath. "In fact, when Helen found out that Grant and I had visited the clinic, she tried to bribe one of the nurses to get info about what we were doing. When I found out, I had our counselor put a note in my file that no information should be given to the woman."

"That doesn't mean Helen played by the rules," Drury reminded her. In fact, he'd be surprised if she had. But there was someone else in that scummy family who was also a rule breaker. "What about Grant's brother, Jeremy?"

Drury couldn't be sure, but he thought Caitlyn shuddered. "Jeremy wouldn't have done that. And yes, I'm sure. The last thing Jeremy would want is another heir to share the inheritance he'll get from his mother."

"Okay," Grayson said, "this is enough to get things started. How far out are you now?"

"About ten minutes. No one's following us, but when we get to the sheriff's office, I want to get Caitlyn and the baby inside ASAP."

"No problem. Park right in front of the door."

Drury hit the end-call button and took another glance back at her. "I know you don't want to go to the sheriff's office, but you can trust Grayson. If there's anything to link Helen to this, he'll find it."

And so would Drury. He hadn't especially wanted to get involved with Caitlyn, but this wasn't about her. It was about that baby in her arms.

"You think I'm a fool for getting involved with Grant," she said. "But I swear, I didn't know what Grant was when I married him."

"You should have. You knew what his family was, knew that I was investigating them."

"Yes," she whispered. And she repeated it. "His

family but not him." She paused. "I think Jeremy might have been the one who killed Grant."

"Killed? I thought he died in a car accident."

"He did. One that Jeremy could have arranged." Though she shook her head right after saying that. "I don't have any proof, and knowing Jeremy, there won't be proof to find. But I meant what I said about Jeremy not wanting any competition for his mother's estate."

The last time he'd tangled with the Densons, he hadn't fared so well. Drury had ended up with a black mark on his reputation for getting involved with Caitlyn, a woman who'd clearly double-crossed him and had almost certainly been sleeping with him to get info about his investigation.

Of course, that hadn't stopped Drury from trying to go after the Densons again. Until his boss had finally gotten him to back off when Helen had threatened a lawsuit for harassment. Drury hadn't wanted to hurt the Bureau for what had essentially become a personal vendetta on his part.

"I hate being drawn back into the viper pit." He hadn't intended to say that loud enough for Caitlyn to hear.

But she heard. Because she gave him another "I'm sorry."

He kept the next comment to himself. Was she sorry she'd dumped him for Grant? Or sorry that she hadn't gotten that safe fairy tale that she wanted?

Drury wanted to tell her that she couldn't create "safe." The cut on her head and baby in her arms were proof of that. Still, he couldn't fault her for trying. After all, she'd seen her own father—a Texas Ranger—gunned down right in front of her when she was only eight.

Hard to get past memories like that.

Drury took the final turn toward town, and he tried to shut out everything so he could focus on their surroundings. It was late, nearly midnight, and with the rain there wasn't anyone out and about. Still, those thugs could be waiting on a side street, watching for them.

He held his breath and didn't release it until he saw the sheriff's office. And Grayson in the doorway. The moment Drury had brought the car to a stop, Grayson hurried Caitlyn inside, and Drury followed right behind her. He got her away from the windows—fast. Even though they were bullet resistant, he didn't want to take any chances.

After everything that'd gone on, Drury hadn't expected a warm greeting from Grayson and Mason. And he didn't get one. Mason was on the phone, scowling. But then, that was something Mason did a lot.

However, Grayson was scowling, too.

At Caitlyn.

"Is there any part of your story you want to re-think?" Grayson asked her.

That put some alarm in her eyes, and Caitlyn shook her head. "No. Why?"

"Because I just got off the phone with the doctor who's patching up Ronnie Waite, and Ronnie says that's his daughter and that you kidnapped her. He's demanding a warrant for your arrest."

Chapter Four

Caitlyn felt as if someone had knocked the breath right out of her. She shook her head, tried to deny what Ronnie had claimed, but the words were trapped in her throat.

"Is it true?" Grayson snapped.

It was more of an accusation than a question, and Caitlyn was thankful it had come from Grayson and not Drury. Still, that didn't mean Drury believed she was innocent. He was staring at her, clearly waiting for her to say something.

"Everything happened just the way I told you," she insisted.

Drury just kept staring, but Grayson made a sound, one to let her know she was going to have to do a whole lot better than that if he was to believe her.

"The baby isn't his," Caitlyn tried again. "I paid him one ransom, and he demanded a second one. Since I figured he wasn't just going to hand over the baby, I hit him with a stun gun and took her from him."

"I don't suppose you recorded any of that encounter?" Grayson, again. And he used the tone of the lawman in charge. Which he was. He also made this sound, and feel, like an interrogation.

Mercy. If she couldn't convince him of her innocence, he might take the baby. He might arrest her. That couldn't happen because if she was behind bars, she wouldn't be able to protect the baby.

"He clubbed me on the head," Caitlyn added, and she looked to Drury for help. She held her breath, hoping that he would back her up, and he finally nodded.

"When I found Caitlyn in my house, she was scared. And bleeding."

Grayson lifted his shoulder, and even though he didn't say the actual words, his expression was a reminder that she'd fooled Drury before. That's the way the Rylands would see it anyway. But she hadn't fooled him so much as she'd been fooled.

By Grant.

But that was an old wound of a different kind.

"Think this through," Caitlyn continued because she clearly had some more convincing to do with Grayson. "Why would I steal a baby and run to Drury?"

Grayson stayed quiet, probably because there

was no scenario he could come up with where she'd do that. Because she wouldn't.

"So, the baby is really yours?" Grayson asked.

Caitlyn hated to hesitate, but she didn't want to withhold anything. Considering her track record with the Rylands, it would be hard enough to get them to trust her if they caught her in a lie.

She looked down at the newborn. At that precious little face, and she got that same deep feeling of love that she'd gotten the first time she saw her. Of course, she'd been wrong about her feelings before, but Caitlyn didn't think that was the case right now. In fact, she would stake her life on it.

"Other than the test I had run on the DNA sample the kidnapper sent me, I don't have any proof," Caitlyn admitted, "but she looks like the pictures of me when I was a baby."

Grayson groaned, an almost identical reaction to the one Drury had had when she'd first told him.

"I can get the proof," she insisted. "I can have her DNA tested again and compared to mine and Grant's. I just need time." She stepped closer to Grayson and looked him straight in the eyes. "But I'm not going to give her to you so you can hand her over to the very man who tried to kill us."

Grayson's attention shifted to Drury then. "You believe her?"

Drury didn't answer for several long moments. "The guy shot at me when I pulled up in front of my house. If he was truly just after Caitlyn to get his child back, then why go after me like that?" He tapped his badge. "I identified myself, and he still shot at me. Plus, he had those items in his vehicle."

No head shake from Grayson this time. He nodded. Apparently, that was enough to convince him that Ronnie was lying.

"I'll post a deputy outside his hospital room and keep digging into his background to see what turns up," Grayson said. "Why don't you two wait in my office while I call the doctor and get him down here?"

Caitlyn wasn't sure she could trust the doctor. Any doctor. But her options were limited. She couldn't just go running out into the rainy night with the baby, and she didn't even have any supplies.

"Could you please have someone get the baby some formula and diapers?" she asked.

Another nod from Grayson, and he got started on that while Drury led her to Grayson's office. It wasn't the first time she'd been there. Once when she'd still been seeing Drury, he'd brought her here to meet his cousins. Of course, they had been a lot friendlier to her than they were now.

Because her legs felt ready to give way, Caitlyn sank down into one of the chairs and looked up at Drury. "Thank you."

He huffed, clearly not meant to convey "you're welcome" because he probably hated her for getting him involved in this. Maybe soon she could convince him that she truly was sorry along with making plans to put some distance between them.

But how?

She didn't even have a phone, and besides even if she had one, Caitlyn wasn't sure who to call. Maybe a bodyguard, but at this point, she didn't even know who she could trust.

Other than Drury, that is.

And that trust was on shaky ground. Yes, he would protect her because he was an FBI agent and it was his job, but she'd already put him in danger once and didn't want to risk doing that again.

"Can you help me arrange for a safe house?" she asked.

A muscle flickered in his jaw, and he pulled a chair from the corner and sat where he was facing her. "Yes, I can do that, but I want you to do something for me. Tell me everything—and I mean everything—about who could be part of this."

Caitlyn was certain she looked confused. Because she was. "You mean about the baby?"

"For starters. You didn't have anything to do with what went on at Conceptions, did you?"

That put a huge knot in her stomach. Not because it was true. It wasn't. But because he would even consider she'd do something like that.

"No. I gave up on having Grant's baby months before he died." And she made the mistake of dodging his gaze.

Drury noticed.

He put his fingers beneath her chin, lifting it and forcing eye contact. "Explain that," he insisted.

Caitlyn hadn't wanted to get into all of this now, but it could be connected. *Could.* Still, it would mean reopening old wounds that still hadn't healed. Never would. Plus, it was hard to discuss any of this when she was holding the baby. Perhaps Grant's and her baby.

"When Grant was killed, he'd been having an affair," she said.

"Is that the reason you were divorcing him?"

"Among other things." Caitlyn paused. "The only reason I'm bringing it up now is because his girlfriend, Melanie Cordova, could be responsible for at least part of this."

Of course, he looked confused, and Drury motioned for her to continue.

Caitlyn did, after she took a deep breath. "Melanie was devastated after Grant's death, and it's possible she's the one who arranged for the baby to be born. So she could have some part of Grant."

"Even if that *part* meant the baby would be yours?" he questioned. "Because as a mistress, you'd think the last thing she would want around was her lover's baby with another woman."

"I know," Caitlyn admitted. Obviously, there were holes in her theory about Melanie's possible involvement. "But maybe Melanie was so desperate to have Grant's child that she didn't care if I was the biological mother."

Judging from the way his forehead bunched up, Drury clearly wasn't on board with this. "Then why would Melanie have demanded a ransom? Why even let you know that the child existed?"

Caitlyn had to shake her head. "Unless she just wanted the money to raise the baby. Of course, that doesn't explain why that thug Ronnie had her."

"Maybe that wasn't Melanie's choice. If she hired him to extort the ransom, he could have double-crossed her and kidnapped the baby."

Mercy. Caitlyn hadn't even thought of that. Maybe this was a sick plan that had gone terribly wrong.

"How long has it been since you've seen Melanie?" Drury asked. "Is it possible she carried the baby herself, that she's the surrogate?"

It was yet something else Caitlyn hadn't considered, but she had to nod. "I haven't seen her in over a year. For a few months after Grant died, she stalked me. Followed me, kept calling, that sort of thing, but that all stopped about a year ago."

Perhaps around the time Melanie would have been arranging for the procedure to have the baby.

Caitlyn didn't have to ask how Melanie would have gotten the fertilized embryo from Conceptions. She could have bribed someone in the clinic, possibly even the former clinic manager who'd orchestrated several births just so she could extort money from the babies' biological parents. Something that Drury knew all too well.

Since two of those babies were his twin niece and nephew.

The clinic manager was dead now, killed in a gunfight with Drury's brother Holden so she couldn't give them answers, but it was possible that Melanie could.

Drury stood. "I'll make some calls and get Melanie in for questioning."

He took out his phone, but before he could do anything, Grayson stepped into the doorway. One look at his face, and Caitlyn knew something was wrong.

"Ronnie called Child Protective Services," Grayson said. "He wants the baby in their custody."

That robbed Caitlyn of her breath, and she stood, as well. She also pulled the baby even closer to her. "It's some kind of trick. Ronnie probably figures it'll be easier to snatch the baby from foster care than from me."

Grayson made a sound of agreement. "But that won't stop CPS from taking her. They're on their way here now."

Caitlyn would have bolted for the door if Drury hadn't stopped her. No. This couldn't be happening.

"If I let them take the baby, it'd be like giving her back to Ronnie," Caitlyn pleaded. "I can't do that."

She braced herself for an argument, but one didn't come.

"Ronnie tried to kill me," Drury reminded Grayson. "Anything he does is suspect, and Caitlyn is right. He or one of his thug friends would have a much easier time getting the baby from CPS. In fact, the plan could be to kidnap her as soon as she's taken from the building."

Still no argument from Grayson, but he did stay quiet a moment. Before he nodded. "I don't trust Ronnie, either. Or rather I don't trust the person he's working for." Grayson looked at Caitlyn. "That still doesn't mean I can give you a blank check on this. How much time will you need to prove she's your daughter?"

Caitlyn had to shake her head. "How much time for you to arrange another DNA test, one that would hold up against a court order?"

"Forty-eight hours, maybe even sooner, if we put a rush on it," Drury answered. "We'll need the lab you used to process Grant's DNA, though."

Yes, because she didn't want to take the time to try to find another hair sample. "I used Biotech in San Antonio. They'll have both Grant's and my DNA on file there."

She could see the debate Grayson was having with himself. He was a lawman. A good one, judging from everything she'd heard. And it likely didn't set well with him that this would essentially be an obstruction of justice since he was allowing Caitlyn to walk away with the baby rather than turning her over to CPS.

"All right," Grayson finally said. "Forty-eight hours. I'll get the DNA test kit. After that, go ahead and get Caitlyn and her out of here."

The relief was instant, and it left her just as breathless as the news of Ronnie calling CPS. She wasn't going to have to give up the baby. Not just yet anyway. But that didn't mean she had a safe place to take her.

"Where?" she asked Drury and hoped he had some idea.

"Don't tell me where you're going," Grayson quickly added. "I don't want to have to lie to CPS. Oh, and figure out how the baby can get a checkup from the doctor." He walked away, no doubt to get that kit.

She certainly hadn't forgotten about the checkup but didn't know how to make it happen.

"It's not a good idea to go back to my place," Caitlyn insisted before Drury could say anything. "Or yours."

"Agreed. But there's a guesthouse on the back part of the ranch. It's out of sight from the other houses, including Grayson's, and we can use it just for tonight. Since my cousins have lots of babies, it'll be easier for us to get supplies."

"It'll also make them a target if Ronnie and his goon friends attack again," she quickly pointed out.

"We can lock down the ranch, close the security gate and use some of the hands for extra protection."

Maybe, but Caitlyn still wasn't sold on the idea. *Think.* Where else could she go? And preferably some place that didn't put others in danger.

"It's just for tonight," Drury said as if he knew what was going through her mind. "The baby will need to be fed soon, and it won't be long before CPS arrives."

True. Still, Caitlyn didn't like it one bit.

"Are you, uh, okay with this?" But she immediately waved off her question. "Of course you're not okay. First thing in the morning, I promise, I'll start looking for bodyguards."

He didn't give her his opinion on that. "I'll pull an unmarked car to the back of the building."

Drury headed out as Grayson came in with the DNA test kit. He'd obviously done this before because he did the cheek swab in just a few seconds. The baby still stirred a little and made a whimpering sound of protest, but she went right back to sleep.

"I'll have this couriered to the lab," Grayson explained as he started toward the door again. But he stopped. "If the child's not yours, I'll expect you to turn her over to CPS. Got that?"

She nodded. Caitlyn understood that's what would have to happen. Well, she understood with her head anyway. It was her heart that was giving her some trouble because Caitlyn felt as if this baby already belonged to her. It would crush her to learn differently.

Caitlyn heard the footsteps in the hall and automatically tensed, but it was just Drury. He glanced at the DNA packet.

"I'll call you as soon as we have the results," Grayson assured them.

Drury took her by the arm and led her to the back of the building and through a break room. He paused at the exit, opening the door and glancing around. He also drew his weapon before he helped her out and into the backseat of the waiting unmarked car.

Which wasn't empty.

Drury's brother Lucas was behind the wheel.

"Lucas came when he heard about the attack," Drury said.

Since Lucas was a Texas Ranger, it made sense that he would know about the attack, but it surprised her that he would involve himself in this. Like most of the Rylands, Lucas disliked her, maybe even hated her, because of the nasty breakup between Drury and her.

Lucas didn't say a word to her, though he did spare her a glance in the rearview mirror. He took off as soon as Drury had shut the door.

Drury kept his gun drawn, and he looked all around them. No doubt for any thugs who might be watching for them to leave.

Suddenly, a new wave of fear crawled through her. As bad as it'd been inside the sheriff's office, this was worse.

"Is the car bulletproof?" she asked, and she hated the tremble in her voice.

"Bullet resistant," Drury corrected.

She wasn't certain, but Caitlyn thought that meant they could still be shot. Drury was certainly aware of that possibility, too. And this had to be bringing back god-awful memories for him.

"I'm sorry," she said.

There was no way Drury could have known what the blanket apology meant. Or at least she hadn't thought he would know, but when he glanced at her, she saw it in his eyes. The memories.

Or rather the nightmare.

Of his wife. Lily. She'd been killed by a gunman's bullet in a botched store robbery, and while Caitlyn didn't know all the details, she knew Drury had still been grieving her loss when they'd met. Heck, he probably still was.

And she hadn't helped with that.

Just as Drury had started to risk his heart again, she'd stomped on it. It didn't matter that she thought she had a good reason. Several of them in fact. No. It didn't matter.

Drury's phone buzzed, and Caitlyn prayed this wasn't another round of bad news. However, that wasn't a bad news kind of look on Drury's face when he looked at the screen.

"Don't say anything," he warned her. He pressed the answer button and put the call on speaker.

It didn't take long for her to hear the caller's voice. "What the hell did you do?" the man asked.

Caitlyn immediately recognized the voice, and it only tightened the knot in her stomach. Because it was her former brother-in-law and one of her suspects.

Jeremy.

"Well?" Jeremy snapped when Drury didn't immediately answer.

"Well what?" Drury snapped right back.

"You know. You damn well know."

Drury huffed. "I'm giving you one more chance to make sense, and if you don't, I'm ending this call. Then you can bother someone else. What is it that you think I did?"

"You sent those men after me," Jeremy insisted.

Drury looked at Caitlyn, no doubt to see if she knew anything about this, but she shook her head.

"What men?" Drury questioned.

"The men who want money. A ransom, they said. They want me to pay them for Grant's kid."

It took Caitlyn a moment for that to sink in. Had the kidnappers really contacted Jeremy? If so, they'd probably done the same to his mother, too. Of course, that was assuming that Jeremy was telling the truth, but Caitlyn didn't trust him. Trusted his mother even less.

Drury cursed. "Start talking, and tell me everything," he ordered Jeremy.

"I've already told you everything. Two men showed up at my office a couple of minutes ago. Or rather the parking lot at my office. They accosted me, showed me a picture of some kid that they claimed was Grant and Caitlyn's."

"Who were the men?" Drury pressed. "And where are they now?"

"I don't know. Never saw them before in my life. But they said something about the kid being born through a surrogate and if I wanted the kid that I was to pony up a million bucks. They said I had one hour to get the cash, and they left. They drove off in a black SUV."

"I'm still trying to figure out why you think I had anything to do with this," Drury said.

Jeremy made a sound to indicate that the answer was obvious. It wasn't. "The men told me to pay the money to you."

Because Drury's arm was touching hers, she felt his muscles tense. "Me?"

But Jeremy didn't jump to verify that. Instead, he cursed. "The men are back."

Caitlyn heard some shouts, one of them belonging to Jeremy. "Stop!" he yelled.

"Get someone out to Jeremy Denson's office," Drury told his brother. "Jeremy, are you there?"

No answer.

The line was dead.

Chapter Five

Drury waited. Something he'd been doing all night.

Patience had never been his strong suit, and that was especially true now. He wanted answers. Answers that he wasn't getting. Well, he wasn't getting the right answers anyway.

He'd certainly gotten a string of wrong ones.

No news on Jeremy. Nothing else on the kidnappers, either. Ronnie was sticking to his story about Caitlyn stealing his child. And CPS was pushing Grayson to disclose the location of the baby.

Grayson was staying quiet for now on anything about the baby, though he almost certainly knew that they were at the ranch. Drury wasn't sure how long Grayson's silence would last. Especially since CPS had said they would get protection for the little girl. If they did that, Drury wasn't even sure it was a good idea for Caitlyn and him to keep her.

Unless the child turned out to be hers, that is.

If the baby was indeed her child, then there was no way Caitlyn would give her up. A match wouldn't mean the baby was safe, though. Caitlyn, either. And that left Drury with another question for which he didn't have an answer.

What then?

The logical part of him was saying he should step away from this. That his past with Caitlyn was just that—the past. But the illogical part of him put up an argument about it. Drury figured it had plenty to do with the old attraction. The one that was still there.

He threw back the covers and got off the sofa where he'd spent the night. Not sleeping, that's for sure. The sofa was about six inches too short for his body, and the thoughts racing through his head hadn't exactly spurred a peaceful sleep. He could still hear the shots. Could still see that look of terror on Caitlyn's face.

Of course, the shooting had brought back the old memories. Of that same look of terror on Lily's face before she'd died in his arms. Memories that he pushed aside. Like the attraction for Caitlyn, he didn't want to cloud his mind with things from the past that he couldn't change.

Since he didn't hear Caitlyn stirring in the bedroom, he tried to be quiet when he went to the kitchen and made some coffee. The small counter was dotted with baby formula and other supplies. Something Lucas had managed to get for them before he'd left the guesthouse shortly after midnight. Later, Drury would need to thank him for helping. Grayson, too.

And that thanks would include them not mentioning that he shouldn't be under the same roof with Caitlyn.

Drury sipped his coffee, went through his emails on the laptop that Lucas had also provided. No updates since the last time he checked other than Grayson was going to have the deputy at the hospital talk to Ronnie again. Maybe the man would cave on his story so that there'd be no question about Caitlyn's innocence.

She already had enough strikes against her with his family of lawmen without adding that.

He heard a slight thudding sound in the bedroom, and Drury practically threw his coffee cup on the table and hurried to find out if anything had happened. Not that he had to go far. It was literally only a few steps from the kitchen. He drew his gun from his shoulder holster and threw open the door, bracing himself for the worst. But it wasn't the *worst*.

Caitlyn was standing there naked.

Almost naked anyway. She was putting on an

oversize bathrobe, and he got a glimpse of her body before she managed to yank the sides together and tie the sash.

"Sorry," she whispered. Maybe an apology for the peep show. Or maybe because she'd clearly startled him. Caitlyn picked up the plastic baby bottle that she'd obviously dropped. "I'm on edge, too," she added.

No doubt, but at the moment she didn't exactly look on edge. Their gazes connected. Held. And he saw in her eyes something he didn't want to see. The old heat.

Drury looked away and reholstered his gun. Since he was already there, he also checked on the baby. There'd been no time to get a crib, so the little girl was sleeping on the center of the bed where she'd likely spent most of the night. The covers on the floor told him that Caitlyn had probably slept there.

"I was afraid of rolling onto her during the night," Caitlyn said. "She's so little." There was some fear in her voice, but he didn't think it was from the danger but rather because it was true. The baby really was tiny.

"Did she sleep okay?" he asked.

Caitlyn nodded, then shrugged. "I guess she did. I don't really know how often a baby should be waking up."

Neither did Drury, but Caitlyn had gotten up

twice in the night to warm bottles. Drury had asked if he could help. Especially since Caitlyn had had to walk right past him to get to the kitchen. But she'd declined his offer.

"Please tell me you have good news. *Any* good news," Caitlyn said.

It took Drury a couple of moments to come up with something that could possibly be considered good. "Grayson is bringing in both Helen and Melanie for questioning."

Caitlyn flexed her eyebrows. "I'm betting neither was happy about that."

"They weren't. Especially Helen. Grayson said she didn't seem too concerned when he told her about the call we'd gotten from Jeremy."

"She wouldn't be. Jeremy and she haven't been on friendly terms in years. Jeremy's a hothead."

Yeah, Drury had figured that out from the brief phone call. But the "hothead" was about to be labeled a missing person if they didn't hear from him soon.

"Someone had tampered with the security cameras in the parking garage where Jeremy made that call," he explained. "There's no footage for fifteen minutes before the call or for a half hour afterward."

She stayed quiet a moment. "You think Jeremy could have really been kidnapped?"

Drury had to lift his shoulder. "You know him better than I do. Would he fake a disappearance?"

"Yes," Caitlyn said without hesitation. "If it benefited him in some way. And this possibly could if he thought he was a suspect in the attack last night." But then she shook her head. "Of course, he wouldn't have had any part in her birth." She glanced at the baby.

"Because he wouldn't want to share his inheritance." Drury remembered Caitlyn mentioning that. "But if he's worried about splitting an inheritance, wouldn't he try to smooth things over with his mom?"

"Helen can't cut him out of the estate. That's in the terms of his late father's will. Jeremy will inherit everything unless Grant has an heir."

Drury figured the estate had to be worth millions. Still, it took a coldhearted SOB to go after a child because of money. If that's what Jeremy had done. Considering the bad blood between him and his mother, Helen might have used this as an opportunity to get rid of Jeremy, her sole surviving son.

Especially if the woman thought she had a new heir. Grant's baby.

"I was about to take a shower." Caitlyn fluttered her fingers toward the adjoining bathroom. "That's why I wasn't dressed when you came in.

I was going to put her in the carrier on the bathroom floor, but could you watch her?"

Drury nodded. And hoped the baby didn't wake
up. Unlike his cousins, he just wasn't comfortable
holding a newborn.

"I won't be long," Caitlyn added, and she hurried into the bathroom.

He sank down on the edge of the bed and studied the little girl's face. He could see Caitlyn's
mouth and chin. Or at least he thought he could.
No resemblance to Grant, though, and it surprised
him a little to realize that even if he had seen it,
it wouldn't have made him uneasy. His beef had
never been with Grant.

But rather Caitlyn leaving him to be with Grant.

Of course, it was his own stupid fault for handing Caitlyn his heart when he knew he was the
wrong man for her. She'd told him right from the
get-go that she couldn't get involved with a lawman. Not after her lawman father's violent death.
Even after they'd started an affair, she had continued to tell Drury that it could never be more
than temporary between them.

Too bad he hadn't believed her.

Caitlyn was right about not being too long. She
stayed in the shower only a couple of minutes, and
it took her even less than that to dress. She hurried out while combing her wet hair.

She smelled like roses.

The soap, no doubt, but it was something he wished he hadn't noticed.

"Thanks," she said.

Since it was time for him to get the heck out of the bedroom, Drury stood, but the moment he did, the baby squirmed a little and made a fussing sound. He stepped back so that Caitlyn could go to her and take her in her arms.

They made a picture together. And Drury had no trouble seeing the love for the child in Caitlyn's eyes.

"I know," Caitlyn said, following his gaze to the baby. "I shouldn't get so attached. But I've always wanted a child, so it's hard not to have deep feelings for her."

An understatement. Caitlyn had *really* wanted a child. Something she'd made clear when they were together.

Something that had driven a wedge between them, too.

Heck, it still made him take a step back now.

Too many memories. More of those old ones that he wanted to forget. But couldn't. Because he hadn't just lost his wife the day she'd been murdered. He'd lost the child that she'd been carrying.

"Will you still help me with a safe house?" she asked. "An unofficial one, of course. I don't think you want to use FBI channels."

Neither did he. "I'll help with the house." Hell,

he'd ended up helping with plenty of things he didn't want to help with, but despite their past he was still a sucker for a damsel in distress, and at the moment Caitlyn was in a lot of *distress*.

She mumbled another thanks. "I was going to get started on contacting some bodyguards, and I was hoping I could use your laptop to get some phone numbers."

He nearly offered her a protection detail. But he was also toeing the line on the law. Heck, he'd probably crossed over that line, and he didn't want to bring any of his fellow agents or family into this.

"The laptop's on the table in the kitchen," he said.

She gathered the blanket around the baby and headed that direction. Drury followed, but before he even made it there, his phone buzzed, and he saw Grayson's name on the screen. He considered not putting the call on speaker, just in case this was more bad news, but he'd end up telling Caitlyn about the conversation anyway.

"You're on speaker," Drury warned Grayson right off, though he doubted that would change anything Grayson had to say.

"Good. Because Caitlyn needs to hear this. I've arranged for the doctor to examine the baby. Yeah, I know. It's a risk, but she needs to be checked out."

"I agree." A weary sigh left Caitlyn's mouth. "And it's something I should have remembered to do."

"You've had a lot on your mind lately." There was a touch of sarcasm in Grayson's tone. "I want you two to take the baby to the hospital. And don't worry, she won't be near Ronnie. The doctor will meet you in his private office to do the exam. I've arranged for Lucas and one of the deputies to escort you there."

Escort was a nice way of saying *back up* in case someone tried to gun them down again.

"Anything new from Ronnie?" Drury asked.

"Nothing. He's lawyered up and is refusing to cooperate with us. Not CPS, though. He's still pressuring them to give him the baby. Which they won't do," Grayson quickly added. "Not without DNA proof anyway, and it'll be tomorrow before we have that."

"The DNA will show that Ronnie's not the father," Caitlyn said like gospel, and Drury hoped that was true.

He didn't exactly relish the idea of handing over a child to someone who'd shot at him. Of course, that wouldn't happen anyway unless Ronnie was cleared of all charges.

"Ronnie said he can prove the baby is his," Grayson went on. "Because he can describe the birthmark on her ankle. Does she have a birthmark?"

"She does," Caitlyn admitted. "But Ronnie could have easily seen it when he had her."

"That was my theory, too. By the way, Melanie's on her way in," Grayson added a moment later. "Drury, if you want to be here for the interview, you could have Lucas or someone else stay with Caitlyn and the baby."

It was tempting. "When will she be there?" Drury asked.

"Within the hour." He paused. "I have plenty of questions for her now that I've read the police report for Grant's car accident. Melanie's purse was found in the vehicle."

Drury had read the report, too. Not recently. But shortly after Grant had died. Why? He didn't know. It was a way of picking at those old wounds, but he hadn't been able to stop himself. So, yeah, he knew about Melanie's purse.

Obviously so did Caitlyn. "Melanie claimed that Grant and she had been together that night, but when he dropped her off at her place, she forgot her purse." She frowned. "The police cleared her as a suspect, but you think Melanie could have had something to do with his death?"

"Do you?" Grayson asked right back.

She certainly didn't jump to deny it. Caitlyn took a moment and gently rocked the baby even though the little girl was no longer fussing. "Possibly. Jeremy is still my top suspect for that. If it wasn't an accident, that is. But I suppose Melanie could have been upset with Grant about something."

"You don't know?" Grayson pressed.

"No. By then Grant and I were separated. That's why I was a suspect at first, but I was cleared, too, because it was ruled an accident. Added to that, I had an alibi."

"A ruptured appendix," Drury mumbled.

Caitlyn's gaze raced to his, and she looked a little surprised that he knew that. When it came to her, Drury always seemed to know a little too much. Like that she'd nearly died herself that night and was in emergency surgery at the same time her estranged husband swerved off the road and hit a tree. Since there'd been other skid marks nearby, the cops had first thought someone had run him off the road, but the CSIs hadn't been able to prove that the marks were made the exact same time as the accident.

"I just want to know as much about Melanie as possible before I question her," Grayson went on. "Does she have any hot buttons?"

"Me," Caitlyn answered. "Until I filed for divorce, she was harassing me. She hates me. That's why I told Drury that I didn't think she had anything to do with the baby or Conceptions Clinic."

Grayson made a sound to indicate he was withholding judgment on that. "I'll let you know if I find out anything from her, and I'll have Lucas give you a call once he's on his way there. By the way, Lucas didn't tell me exactly where you were on the ranch, and I'd like to keep it that way."

So would Drury. The fewer people who knew, the better.

Drury ended the call, and since Caitlyn had said she wanted to use his laptop, he turned it in her direction. She glanced at the baby. Then at him.

"I'll get the carrier from the bedroom," she said, not giving him a chance to decline to hold the baby. Not that he would have. But Caitlyn must have realized that it wasn't something he wanted to do.

Several moments later, she came back into the kitchen, the baby already snuggled into the carrier, and she set the carrier on the table next to the laptop.

"For a bodyguard search, try starting with Sencor Agency in San Antonio," he suggested.

She muttered a thanks and got started on that just as Drury's phone buzzed again. Not Grayson this time but rather his brother Mason, who lived at the main house on the ranch.

"We have a visitor," Mason growled the moment Drury answered. "She's at the security gate pitching a fit. I didn't tell her either of you were here, but she's insisting on seeing Caitlyn."

Even though Drury didn't have the phone on speaker, either Caitlyn heard or else she noticed the alarm on Drury's face because she slowly got to her feet.

"Who is it? Melanie?" Drury asked.

"No. It's Caitlyn's mother-in-law, Helen. And along with demanding to see Caitlyn, she says she wants her grandbaby right now."

Chapter Six

Caitlyn squeezed her eyes shut a moment. This was the last thing she'd expected—for Grant's mother to show up at the Silver Creek Ranch.

"How did Helen know Caitlyn was here?" Drury asked, taking the question right out of her mouth.

Of course, Caitlyn had an even more important question. How had Helen found out about the baby?

"She said a man called her," Mason answered. "Ronnie Waite. He told her that Caitlyn would be here."

Caitlyn had to shake her head. "Why would Ronnie have done that? He's claiming the baby is his."

"Yeah, apparently your mother-in-law doesn't believe that."

"Former mother-in-law," Caitlyn automatically corrected.

Mason grumbled something that sounded like a *whatever.* "She's on hold on the house line if you want to have a little chat with her. If not, I'll have the ranch hands *escort* her off the property."

Helen wouldn't go peacefully. She didn't do much in life that qualified as peaceful. And Caitlyn didn't want the Rylands or their ranch hands to have to deal with the woman. Heck, she didn't want to deal with Helen, either, but the fastest way to get rid of her might be to take the call.

"I'll speak to her," Caitlyn volunteered.

"Not a smart idea," Drury snapped. "It'll confirm to her that you're here."

"I can tell her that I transferred the call to your location," Mason suggested. "I won't have to tell her where, exactly, that location is."

"Yes, please do that," Caitlyn said, ignoring Drury's huff. She picked up the landline phone and waited.

Despite Drury not agreeing to this, he used the laptop to tap into the ranch's security system. There were multiple screens, and he zoomed in on the one at the security gate. Helen was there all right, her phone pressed to her ear while she glared at the two armed ranch hands who were blocking her from getting past the gate.

Helen was aware of the camera because she was volleying glances between it and the ranch hands. The October wind had kicked up some and was rifling through her blond hair. Hair that was usually perfect. Ditto for her dark jacket, but she definitely looked a little disheveled this morning.

At least the baby had fallen back to sleep and Helen wouldn't be able to hear her, but just in case she woke up, Caitlyn would keep her voice soft. Also for the baby's sake, she would make this conversation short.

"Start talking," Caitlyn *greeted* Helen the moment the woman came on the line.

"No, you start talking. Tell these goons to let me onto the ranch so I can see the baby."

"We're not at the ranch," Caitlyn lied. "So, you need to leave before they arrest you. It's not very smart to go to a ranch with a family of lawmen and start making a scene."

"It's not right for you to withhold my granddaughter from me," Helen countered. "Did you think you could hide her?"

Caitlyn took a moment to consider her answer, but a moment was too long because Drury took the phone from her and put it on speaker. "What did Ronnie tell you?" he demanded.

"Special Agent Drury Ryland, I presume?" Helen spat out his name like profanity. "Ronnie said you'd be with Caitlyn, that you were helping her hide the baby."

"No, I'm helping her stay alive. Someone tried

to kill the baby and her last night. What do you know about that?"

Helen gasped. Shocked, or else faking that she was. "The baby was in danger?"

"Not what you'd planned, huh?" Drury asked. "Did you tell Ronnie not to fire shots around the baby?"

Since Drury had just accused Helen of hiring a thug like Ronnie to get the baby and kill Caitlyn, it wasn't much of a surprise that her eyes narrowed to slits.

"I know what you're doing," Helen said. "You're trying to put the blame on me for this. Well, I didn't do it. Hell, I didn't even know I had a grandchild until this morning when he called me."

"And did he tell you that the child was his?" Caitlyn countered.

"He said it was possibly his. Or my granddaughter. But he said the odds are that she was Grant's daughter."

Caitlyn groaned. The man was playing both sides.

"What did he want in exchange for the information he was giving you?" Drury asked.

Helen paused. No, it was a hesitation. "He wants me to help him get out of any possible charges that might be filed against him."

"He shot at me, and I won't be giving him a get-out-of-jail-free card on that," Drury stated. "Now tell me everything you know about Ronnie and Conceptions Clinic."

Caitlyn expected the woman to launch into a verbal tirade and blast Drury for the order. She didn't. Helen pushed her hair from her face and sighed.

"I did go to Conceptions," Helen finally admitted. "Not recently, but I went there when Grant told me that Caitlyn was having her eggs harvested. I wanted to find out more about the procedure."

Caitlyn knew Helen well enough to know that she was leaving something out of that explanation. And she thought she might know exactly what.

"You tried to bribe someone into stopping the in vitro," Caitlyn said. Yes, it was a bluff, but she knew she'd hit pay dirt when again Helen didn't jump to deny it.

Helen glanced away from the camera, but her defiance quickly returned. "I knew your marriage to Grant wouldn't last. You weren't in love with him, and he was seeing another woman. That bimbo, Melanie."

Not defiance that time but anger. Apparently, Melanie and Helen had clashed. Or maybe Helen blamed Melanie in some way for her son's death.

"No one at the clinic would listen to me," Helen went on. "And then Grant died and I forgot all about Conceptions."

"Really?" Drury challenged. "You're sure you didn't arrange to use their stored embryo so you could have a grandchild?"

"No." Helen was adamant about it, too. "I had nothing to do with that. But someone must have seen this as a way to make some money. They did with others at Conceptions."

They had, and other than his niece and nephew, there'd been another child, as well. One not connected to the Ryland family or Caitlyn.

"You paid them a ransom," Helen snapped. "Didn't you, Caitlyn?"

It was probably a guess on her part, but Caitlyn saw no reason to deny it. "I did. And when Ronnie reneged on the deal, that's when I hit him with a stun gun and took the child." Caitlyn paused long enough to draw in a long breath. "Helen, if you hired him, tell me now because I need to know if there are others who'll try to kidnap the baby."

"I didn't hire him." No hesitation whatsoever. "But if my granddaughter is in danger, I can help."

"She doesn't need your help," Drury fired back.

Judging from the profanity that he mumbled, he hadn't intended to say that. Probably because it sounded as if he was volunteering to make sure she was safe. Caitlyn wouldn't hold him to that, though. As soon as she had a safe place to go, she and the baby would leave.

"You have no right to keep my granddaughter

from me," Helen argued. She didn't wait for either of them to respond. "I know Caitlyn's always been in love with you, but you're not the baby's father. My son is."

Caitlyn tried not to react to that. Hard to do, though, when she felt as if someone had slapped her. It must have felt that way to Drury, too, because he stared at her, mumbled more of that profanity and looked away.

"You went to Conceptions to stop Caitlyn from having Grant's baby," Drury reminded Helen. "Now you want me to believe that you have a right to see a child that you never wanted to exist?"

Helen didn't fire off a quick answer that time. "My son is dead, and this baby is part of him. Part of *me*. You can't stop me from seeing her."

"I can and will if it means keeping her safe," Drury insisted.

"You can't mean that. You really want to protect Grant's child? Any child for that matter."

Caitlyn saw Drury's old wounds rise to the surface. Helen probably knew all about Drury's past. Knew that her comment would pick at those old wounds. And Caitlyn hated the woman for it.

"I'm an FBI agent," Drury finally said. "I'll do my job, and right now my job is protecting Caitlyn and the baby. A baby whose paternity doesn't matter to me because it won't stop me from protecting her. You won't stop me, either."

Helen flinched. "What does that mean? I told you that I want this child. I wouldn't hurt her."

"Then who would?" Drury snapped. "Who would hire a man like Ronnie to kidnap her?"

"I don't know."

"Then guess!" His voice was so loud that it startled the baby.

Drury mumbled an apology, and Caitlyn gently rocked the carrier so the baby would go back to sleep.

"Jeremy," Helen said.

It didn't take Caitlyn any time at all to realize that Helen had just accused her son of some assorted felonies. Or rather she'd *guessed* he was involved.

"You have proof?" Drury asked.

"No." The woman's shoulders dropped. "I'm sure Caitlyn told you all about how much Jeremy hated Grant. I'm sure Caitlyn told you a lot of things. Pillow talk reveals lots of secrets."

Caitlyn had to bite her lip to keep from shouting out a denial that Drury and she were involved again. Besides, Helen wouldn't believe her no matter what she said, especially since Drury and she were under the same roof.

For the moment anyway.

"Why don't you tell me more about Jeremy?" Drury countered. "Is he really missing or did he fake his disappearance?"

"Who knows?" There was no concern in her expression or her tone. She could have been discussing the weather. "I gave up trying to figure Jeremy out a long time ago."

Drury made a sound of disagreement. "And yet you just accused him of attempted murder. Are you sure you're not trying to put the blame on your son so you won't look guilty?"

Helen glanced around, and when she looked back at the camera, Caitlyn could see new resolve in the woman's eyes. "I'm done with this conversation. If you don't let me see my granddaughter, then I'll call your boss and tell him exactly what you're doing."

"Call him," Drury responded.

Obviously, that wasn't the reaction Helen expected because she shot a glare into the camera. "This isn't over," Helen said, and she stormed back to her car, slamming the door once she was inside.

"She means it." Caitlyn eased the baby carrier back onto the table. "Helen will make trouble for you."

Drury kept his attention focused on the screen where they could see Helen driving away. "She'll try."

Yes, and Helen would keep trying until she got what she wanted. But she wouldn't just want the baby if it turned out that she was her granddaughter. Helen would want the baby without Caitlyn in the picture.

Drury glanced at her and no doubt saw that she was trying to blink back tears. "Don't apologize again," he warned Caitlyn.

She did anyway, but she doubted it would be the last of the apologies that she would owe him. Caitlyn sank down in the chair next to him.

"If you're going to talk about those things Helen just said about us, don't bother," Drury added. He dismissed it with a shake of his head.

However, it dismissed nothing for Caitlyn. "I was in love with you when we were together," she said.

Drury didn't dismiss that, but he did stare at her for a long time before he looked away. "Do you really want to dig up these old bones?"

No. But she couldn't seem to stop herself. "We didn't really talk when things ended between us." In fact, Drury hadn't said a word when she'd told him she was leaving. He wasn't saying a word now, either. "I left because I couldn't be there, not after what happened."

There was no reason for her to explain that. Because Drury hadn't forgotten that he'd nearly been killed just the day before she'd ended things. Nearly killed while doing his job.

A job he would never give up.

"I saw the pictures of the attack," she went on.

Again, she didn't need to add to that because he knew which pictures she meant. Drury had been caught in the middle of a gunfight while on a task force to arrest a serial killer, and there'd been bystanders around who'd taken photos that had appeared in every news outlet in the state. On social media, too.

Everywhere she looked, she'd seen Drury on the ground after taking a bullet to the chest. Thankfully, the Kevlar had prevented him from being killed, but he'd had several cracked ribs. Along with escaping death by only a couple of seconds. The killer had taken aim at Drury again, but Drury's partner had stopped him before he could pull the trigger.

In Caitlyn's mind, however, she saw the trigger being pulled. She felt the pain of losing yet another man she loved.

Drury's gaze came back to her. "Is there a reason you're going through all of this now?"

"Yes. I just wanted you to know that it wasn't you. It was me."

For a moment Caitlyn wasn't even sure he was going to acknowledge that. But then he huffed, got to his feet and went to the window.

"We were both in a bad place at that time," he finally said.

Yes, because he was trying to get over the loss of his wife and unborn child. Heck, he was no doubt still trying to get over that. Losing them wasn't a wound that was ever going to heal.

"Does that mean you can forgive me?" she asked.

"No."

Caitlyn had steeled herself up for that answer, but it still cut to the bone. Because it was true.

But Drury waved it off, spared her a glance. "I don't want to forgive you," he amended. "It's easier to hang on to the hurt than it is the pain."

She nodded, and while it wasn't exactly a truce, it was a start. A start that she would take.

His phone buzzed again, and Caitlyn automatically checked the computer screen to make sure Helen hadn't returned. Or that kidnappers hadn't shown up to storm the ranch. But other than the ranch hands, there was no one else at the gate.

"It's Grayson," Drury relayed.

Unlike some of the other calls, he didn't put this one on speaker, and since the air was practically zinging between them, Caitlyn didn't go closer. Best not to risk being so close to him when everything felt ready to explode.

Caitlyn couldn't hear a single word of what Grayson was saying, but she had no trouble interpreting Drury's response. He cursed.

Mercy, what had gone wrong now?

"How did that happen?" Drury snapped.

Again, she couldn't hear Grayson's response.

Whatever it was, though, it didn't help Drury's suddenly tight muscles. It seemed to take an eternity for him to finish the conversation and another eternity before he turned to her.

"Ronnie's gone," he said.

"He escaped?" And her mind automatically thought the worst. That he'd gotten away and was coming after the baby and her. "We should leave now."

Drury shook his head. "He didn't escape. Two men sneaked into the hospital, knocked out the deputy and took him at gunpoint. According to several eyewitnesses, Ronnie's been kidnapped."

Chapter Seven

"I don't like being here," Drury heard Caitlyn say under her breath. She probably hoped that would make the doctor speed up the exam that he was giving the baby.

Drury hoped that as well, but Dr. Michelson sure didn't move any faster. Too bad because being in the hospital was an in-your-face reminder that only a couple of hours earlier, those gunmen had stormed in.

And kidnapped Ronnie.

Well, maybe that's what had happened. But Drury wasn't about to buy it just yet. It was just as likely that Ronnie's comrade-thugs had pretended to take him by force. Or maybe the person who'd hired Ronnie had done that. Not necessarily to rescue him, though, but to silence him after he'd failed to get his hands on the baby.

"There are two deputies outside the door," Drury reminded Caitlyn.

He hadn't figured that would erase the worry on her face. It didn't. Maybe because she remembered that a deputy had been outside Ronnie's room as well, and that hadn't stopped the attack. In fact, the deputy had been hurt. Not seriously. But it could have been a whole lot worse.

"Well, she appears to be fine," the doctor finally said. "Since you don't know the exact day of her birth, I'm estimating that she's at least a week old. She's been well fed, no signs of any kind of injury or trauma."

Caitlyn released the breath that she must have been holding. Of course, Drury had expected the child to be in good health since he hadn't seen any signs to indicate otherwise.

"Can you tell if she was born with a C-section?" Drury asked. "It might make it easier for us to find the surrogate who carried her."

"It's hard to say in her case. Her head is well shaped, which could mean a C-section delivery, but the surrogate could have also had a very short labor. Therefore, the baby wouldn't have been in the birth canal that long."

This seemed like way too much personal information. And it brought back the memories.

Always the memories.

His wife, Lily, had been only three months pregnant when she died, but she'd started reading books about pregnancy and delivery even before they'd conceived. What the doctor had just told him rang some bells. But Drury pushed those bells and memories aside and forced himself to look at the situation from a lawman's point of view.

Basically, the information didn't help at all because it didn't rule out any woman who'd given birth within the past couple of weeks. Plus, Drury figured whoever was responsible for this hadn't delivered the child in a hospital. Too much of a paper trail.

Caitlyn made a sharp sound, and it not only grabbed Drury's attention. It caused him to reach for his gun. False alarm. The sound was the doctor giving the baby a blood test. The baby didn't like it much and kicked and squirmed. Drury figured it was necessary, but he had to look away. Yeah, he was plenty used to seeing blood, but it was different when it was an innocent baby.

"I'll get this to the lab," the doctor said when he finished. Caitlyn immediately got up and scooped the child into her arms.

"I thought you said nothing was wrong with her," Drury reminded him.

"This is just routine, something all newborns have done." Dr. Michelson headed for the door but then stopped. "I won't put your name on it," he said to Caitlyn. "I'll just list it as Baby Ryland. There are enough of those around here that it won't raise any suspicions."

He was right about the sheer number of Rylands, but Drury figured it still might get some attention. The wrong attention, too. That's why Drury didn't want to stick around the hospital much longer. Even though they were in the clinic section, on the other side of the building from where Ronnie had been, that didn't mean someone didn't have the place under surveillance.

"How soon can we leave?" Drury asked the doctor.

"Soon. I just need to get the paperwork for Caitlyn to sign." He headed out, shutting the door behind him.

The baby didn't fuss for long. Probably because Caitlyn was rocking her and looking down at the baby's face with an expression he knew all too well. Love. She'd gotten attached to the child, and that could turn out to be a bad thing if the DNA tests proved the baby belonged to someone else.

But who else?

There'd been no reports of missing newborns in the area, and if the child had been kidnapped from her parents, someone would have almost certainly reported it. If they were still alive, that is.

Caitlyn glanced at him. "I'm sorry about the doctor putting *Ryland* on the lab test."

They were talking about those blasted memories again. The ones Drury didn't want to discuss with her. With anyone.

Instead he took out his phone to make a call about the safe house, but before he could do that, Caitlyn sat down beside him. "I really think you should just walk away from this," she said. "I know how hard this is for you."

Yeah, it was hard, but that pissed him off.

"Walk away? *Right.* I'm a lawman, and even if I weren't, I'm not a coward. There's someone after the baby. Someone who's free as a bird right now." He had to get his teeth unclenched before he could continue. "No, I won't walk away until I'm sure she's safe."

Drury hadn't intended to blurt all that out. Hadn't intended to make a commitment that would keep Caitlyn right by his side. And she would be. Because the baby and Caitlyn were a package deal. At least until the DNA results came back anyway and the person responsible for the danger was caught.

He looked at her and saw that she was staring at him. He also saw just how close they were to each other. Close enough for him to draw in her too-familiar scent. That scent had his number because it slid right through him. Silk and heat.

Apparently, this was his morning for doing things he hadn't planned on doing because he made the mistake of dropping his gaze to her mouth. He remembered how she tasted, knew how it felt to kiss her long and deep.

Worse, his body remembered it, too.

She took in a quick breath, and he saw the pulse flutter on her throat. There was some of that heat in her eyes. Her body seemed to be remembering, as well.

Drury suddenly wanted to kiss her. Or maybe it wasn't so sudden after all. Kissing, and other things, had a way of coming to mind whenever he saw Caitlyn.

He was so caught up in the notion of that kiss that Drury nearly jumped when the sound of his phone startled him. Great. Talk about losing focus.

Grayson's name was on the screen, and Drury pressed the answer button as fast as he could. Maybe his cousin had found something to put an end to all of this.

"Are you still at the hospital?" Grayson asked right off.

"Yeah. But we're nearly finished."

"Good. How would you feel about leaving the baby with the deputies and coming here to the sheriff's office for a short visit?"

"I wouldn't feel good about it at all," Caitlyn answered, which meant she'd heard every word.

Drury put the call on speaker anyway. "What's going on?"

"Melanie's here, and she's in a very chatty mood. Well, up to a point anyway. She's been telling us about Helen's visits to Conceptions, and she claims she knows who Helen might have hired to steal Grant and Caitlyn's embryo."

"She has a name?" Drury quickly asked.

"Says she does, but she's insisting on talking to Caitlyn face-to-face. She says she has questions for her."

Drury didn't want to speculate as to what those questions might be, but he was plenty skeptical that Melanie had any information that would help.

"This could be a ploy to get Caitlyn out into the open," Drury reminded him.

"I know. I could give you a protection detail to get here. A second detail for the baby so she can be taken back to the ranch. But I can't tie up that kind of manpower for long."

No, because that would include four deputies, and that was a third of the lawmen working there.

"You really think my seeing Melanie would help anything?" Caitlyn asked. "And what if CPS finds out I'm there?"

"I can't guarantee you that CPS won't show up, but if they do, I could stall them. As for whether or not Melanie can help, who knows? Right now, I'd like nothing more than to charge her with obstruction of justice for withholding possible evidence, but I doubt I could get the charges to stick.

Melanie could just claim she doesn't have any real info and that she was bluffing so she could speak to Caitlyn."

Drury agreed, and it would also likely rile the woman to the point where she wouldn't give them any info.

"It's your decision," Drury told Caitlyn.

She glanced at the baby, then at Drury before she nodded. "Let's do it," Caitlyn said, getting to her feet.

Drury certainly didn't feel any relief over that decision. Even if Melanie did manage to give them something, it could come at a very high price.

"Go ahead and send the protection details," Drury told Grayson.

"All right… Wait, hold on a second."

Even though there wasn't any alarm in Grayson's voice, Drury went on instant alert. Caitlyn, too. And they waited for several long moments before Grayson finally came back on the line.

"This is apparently the day for surprises," Grayson said. "The cops just found Jeremy."

THE DAY FOR SURPRISES.

Caitlyn hoped Grayson's comment didn't come true in a bad sort of way. It sickened her to think of leaving the baby, even for a short period of time, but that wasn't even her biggest concern.

There could be another attack.

Not only on her, either, but someone could go after the baby while the protection detail was taking her back to the ranch. She hoped they were keeping watch as well as Drury was right now. Though Drury's and her ride was only a short distance, and the ranch was miles away.

"My cousins will protect the baby with their lives," Drury reminded her.

It was the right thing to say, and she believed him. The Rylands might not like her, but they were good lawmen and would do their jobs. Still, that didn't mean the worst couldn't happen, and besides, the visit could all be for nothing. Caitlyn was past the point of having second thoughts about this and had moved on to fourth and fifth thoughts and doubts. That didn't just apply to Melanie.

But to Jeremy.

She listened as Drury got a phone update on the man, and apparently Jeremy had wandered into San Antonio PD with a story about escaping from his kidnappers. Whether that was true or not remained to be seen, but at least now that the cops knew where he was, maybe they could keep an eye on him to make sure he wasn't planning another attack.

"Was Jeremy hurt?" she asked when Drury finished his call.

"Not a scratch on him, but his clothes were disheveled."

Which he could have easily done himself. "How did he *escape*?"

Drury shook his head. "SAPD's questioning him now, and after they're done, they'll send us a copy of the report. In the meantime, we'll deal with Melanie and then head back to the ranch."

That couldn't come soon enough for her. "I'm not even sure why Melanie wants to see me," she said. "If she's really got something dirty on Helen, why wouldn't she just give it to Grayson?"

It was a question she'd already asked herself a dozen times, and she still didn't have an answer.

"Maybe Melanie wants to bargain with you about something," Drury suggested.

She shook her head, not able to imagine what that would be.

"If the baby is Grant's," Drury continued, "maybe she thinks she can convince you to turn the child over to her."

Caitlyn hadn't intended to curse, but the profanity just came out. "No way would I give that woman a baby, any baby."

He lifted his shoulder, continued to glance around as they approached the front of the sheriff's office. "Melanie probably doesn't think too highly of you so she might think she can buy the baby from you."

"She doesn't think much of me, and the feeling's mutual." Caitlyn huffed. "But it does sound like Melanie believes I'd do something that despicable."

The deputy pulled to a stop directly in front of the door to the sheriff's office, and Drury quickly got her inside. He didn't stay at the front with her but rather headed past reception and straight to Grayson's office. Grayson was there, seated at his desk, and he tipped his head to the room across the hall.

"Melanie's in there. Brace yourself," Grayson warned them. "She's a piece of work."

Caitlyn had firsthand knowledge of that, and she tried to look a lot more confident about this meeting than she felt. She wanted only to finish it so she could get back to the baby and complete the plans for a safe house and bodyguards.

When Drury and she walked in, Melanie was seated, her attention on her phone screen, and she barely spared them a glance before continuing to read a text.

"You took your time," Melanie grumbled.

The other times she'd crossed paths with Melanie, the woman had been wearing some high-end outfit suitable for the runway, but today she was wearing skintight jeans and a red top. The heels of her stilettos were no thicker than pencils.

"What did you have to say to me?" Caitlyn asked, and she didn't bother to sound friendly. "I understand you have something on Helen?"

Melanie glanced at her again. A disapproving glance, and as if she had all the time in the world, she got to her feet. With those heels and her height, she towered over Caitlyn and could practically meet Drury eye to eye.

"This is how this will work," Melanie said. "I'll give you some information, and in exchange you'll give me what I want."

Drury's hands went on his hips. "And what exactly is it you want?"

"To do a DNA test on the baby that Caitlyn believes is Grant's and hers."

So, this was about the baby. But Caitlyn certainly hadn't expected Melanie to demand a DNA test.

"What's this about?" Caitlyn pressed.

"It's about giving me a DNA test." She spoke slowly as if Caitlyn were mentally deficient.

Caitlyn had to stop herself from rolling her eyes. "Why don't you explain what you mean?" she asked at the same moment Drury had his own question.

"How did you know about the baby?"

Judging from Melanie's hesitation, that wasn't

something she wanted to answer, but she must have felt she couldn't sidestep it. Not with Drury glaring at her like that.

"Helen," Melanie finally said. "She told me. But it doesn't matter how I found out. This is about what went on at Conceptions." Again, the tone was an attempt to make Caitlyn feel like an idiot. She didn't feel like one, but she was confused. "Helen went to Conceptions to stop Grant and you from having a baby."

"Old news." Caitlyn hoped her own tone made Melanie feel like an idiot. "Helen already admitted that."

Judging from the brief widening of Melanie's eyes, she hadn't expected that. "Did she also tell you that she succeeded, that she did stop it?"

"I stopped it," Caitlyn clarified. "When I filed for a divorce."

"But you think someone else started it again." Melanie wasn't smiling exactly, but it was close. The expression of a woman who had a secret. "Well, you're wrong. No one started it the way you think."

"What the hell are you talking about?" Drury snarled.

With that sly half smile on her face, Melanie sank down onto the chair. "I went to Conceptions, too. Not to stop Caitlyn and Grant's procedure.

Grant had already promised me that he would put a stop to that."

Drury glanced at Caitlyn, no doubt to see if that was true, but she had to shrug. It possibly was. Near the end of their marriage, things hadn't been exactly rosy between Grant and her. Of course, Grant could have lied to his mistress, too.

"I didn't go to Conceptions until after Grant died," Melanie continued. "And I went there to have my eggs harvested. I paid them to use Grant's semen."

"That's illegal," Caitlyn pointed out, but just as quickly, she waved it off. It wouldn't have mattered to Melanie if it was illegal or not. Heck, judging from everything that'd happened at Conceptions, it wouldn't have mattered to them, either.

"I wanted Grant's baby," Melanie said as if that justified everything. "Not yours and his baby. Mine and his."

It took a moment for Caitlyn to find the breath to speak. "Are you saying you think the baby I rescued is yours?"

"Absolutely," Melanie answered without hesitation. "I paid Conceptions to implant mine and Grant's embryo into a surrogate. That's why I'm demanding a DNA test."

Caitlyn felt Drury slip his arm around her waist, and only then did she realize that she wasn't too steady on her feet. "Melanie could be lying," Drury reminded her.

Yes, she could be, but Melanie's smile made Caitlyn think otherwise.

"Why would you use a surrogate?" Drury asked the woman. "Why not just do artificial insemination and carry the baby yourself?"

"Because I have female problems. Not that it's any of your business. Besides, I don't handle pain very well and didn't want to go through childbirth."

And she probably didn't want to risk stretch marks and such on her model-thin figure. In that moment, Caitlyn hated Grant for bringing Melanie into their lives. Hated even more that all of this could be true.

"What's the name of the surrogate?" Drury snapped.

"I don't know. I don't," Melanie repeated when that intensified Drury's glare. "The person at Conceptions told me that had to be kept confidential."

That didn't surprise Caitlyn. Some surrogates would have wanted to keep their identities a secret.

"Even if you paid Conceptions to do the procedure," Drury said, "there are no guarantees that they carried through on it. They were into all sorts of illegal activities and could have just taken your money."

"But there's a baby," Melanie argued.

"A baby that could just as easily be Caitlyn's. After all, the kidnappers contacted her for a ransom. Why wouldn't they have gone to you?"

The smile faded, and Melanie glanced away. "Probably because I'm not loaded like Caitlyn. She's the one who inherited all Grant's money. I didn't get a penny of it."

Yes, and Melanie was just as bitter about that as Helen was. "Did you use your own child to get ransom money from me?" Caitlyn came out and asked.

"No," Melanie practically shouted. But the volume and emotion did nothing to convince Caitlyn that it was true.

God, it could be true.

The baby might not be hers after all. Her stomach knotted and twisted until she felt as if she might throw up.

Drury stared at Melanie. "Let me guess. You think if you have Grant's child that Helen will pony up lots of cash to get shared custody. Or maybe you plan to charge her for visitation rights?"

"That's none of your business. I have my DNA on file at several labs in San Antonio," Melanie went on. "But I don't trust you to tell me the truth.

That's why I want you to bring the baby here so I can watch someone do the test."

"The baby is in protective custody because someone's trying to take her," Drury snapped. "A real mother wouldn't want to put the child in danger by demanding that she be brought here."

That caused Melanie's shoulders to snap back, and she opened her mouth, no doubt ready to argue. But she must have realized just how that would make her look—like the cold, calculating person she was. Plus, if Drury was right about Melanie using the baby to get money from Helen, she wouldn't want to risk her investment being harmed.

"My lawyer will be in touch to schedule that DNA test," Melanie said. "With witnesses. I don't want Caitlyn or any of your cowboy cops trying to pull a fast one on me."

With that accusation, Melanie waltzed out.

Drury kept his arm around her waist, and Caitlyn was thankful for it. Thankful, too, that he'd refused to bring in the baby for testing. Of course, he might not be able to refuse for long. If Melanie had any proof whatsoever that she was the child's mother, then she might be able to get a court order.

"I'll give you two a minute," Grayson said, stepping out and closing the door.

Caitlyn thought she might need more than a minute.

"You okay?" Drury asked her. "Dumb question, I know, but I'm in that gray area where anything I say could make it worse."

She could only shake her head. "Until the kidnapper called me with a ransom demand, it'd been a long time since I'd thought about having a baby. Now, it crushes me to think that I might lose her."

"Yeah." Without taking his arm from her, he stepped in front of her, reached out and touched her cheek. Except he was wiping away a tear. Caitlyn hadn't even realized she was crying until he'd done that.

"Just know that everything Melanie said could be a lie," he continued. "Her story doesn't make sense. She claims she doesn't have money, but she would have needed plenty of cash to bribe someone at Conceptions, plus pay for a surrogate. It's more likely that she tried to get Conceptions to go along with her stupid plan but didn't have the money to put the plan into action."

Caitlyn latched onto that like a lifeline. "Thanks for that."

He nodded but didn't move. Drury stayed put right in front of her. Too close. Well, too close for him anyway, but she wished he would pull her into his arms.

And that's what he did.

Caitlyn stiffened for just a moment from the surprise, but then she felt herself melting right into him. He seemed to do the same against her, and just like that, the memories returned. Good memories, and she had so few of those in her life that it was almost impossible to push them away.

She certainly didn't push Drury away.

Nor did he do any pushing.

He lifted his head a little, their gazes connecting. He was so close to her that she could see the swirls of blue and gray in his eyes. Could see the muscles stirring in his jaw. Drury seemed to be having a fierce debate with himself about something, but Caitlyn didn't know what exactly.

Not until he kissed her, that is.

It barely qualified as a kiss. His mouth just brushed over hers, but his warm breath certainly made her feel as if she'd been kissed.

Now, he stepped back. Cursed. And shook his head. "I just complicated the hell out of this."

"It was already complicated," she assured him.

She figured that wouldn't get any better, either. Drury and she would always have this attraction between them, and because of the past, they would always feel the need to fight it.

"We should get back to the ranch." He didn't wait. Drury headed into the hall but then came to a dead stop.

That's when Caitlyn heard a too-familiar voice.

Jeremy.

He was in the reception area where one of the deputies was frisking him, and the moment she stepped into the squad room, her former brother-in-law spotted her.

"I figured you'd be here," Jeremy snapped. He pointed his finger at Caitlyn. "You want to explain to me why you had me kidnapped?"

Chapter Eight

Drury did not want to have to deal with this now, and he was pretty sure that Caitlyn felt the same way. However, it was clear they were going to have to at least address the stupid accusation Jeremy had just thrown at her.

First, though, Drury had his own issue to address. "Why are you here? Shouldn't you be at San Antonio PD?"

"Not that it's any of your business, but I walked out."

Grayson groaned and took out his phone. No doubt to call his brother Nate, who worked at SAPD, to find out what was going on.

Jeremy flung another pointed finger at Caitlyn. "Now, why did you have me kidnapped?"

"I didn't," Caitlyn answered. "And what makes you think I did?"

Jeremy gave her an annoyed look. "Because one of the kidnappers said you'd hired them."

Caitlyn gave him the look right back. "I didn't hire them, and why would you believe them? They're kidnappers."

"Well, someone kidnapped me, and since whatever's happening seems to be centered on you, that made it easier to believe. That and you hate my guts."

Caitlyn certainly didn't deny the hate part, but she looked at Drury, gave a weary sigh. "Can we leave now?"

Drury nodded and looked at Gage. "Could you bring the car around to the back?" That way, they wouldn't have to go past Jeremy.

Gage returned the nod and headed out of the building. It wouldn't be a fast process, though, because Gage would have to check and make sure no one had planted any kind of tracking device on the vehicle.

"You're not leaving," Jeremy said to Caitlyn. "Not until you tell me who came after me and why."

Caitlyn gave another sigh. "I don't know. The man who tried to kill Drury and me escaped or maybe was taken from the hospital, so I don't have any more answers than you do."

Jeremy disputed that with some ripe profanity. "Then why was that idiot Melanie just here?"

"To be interviewed," Drury stated. He didn't

give Jeremy any more info, something that caused his eyes to narrow.

"Did Melanie have me kidnapped?" Jeremy snarled.

"Maybe. With your personality, I'm surprised half the state doesn't want to kidnap you. Or just shut you up. Now, why would you think Caitlin is involved?" Drury demanded. "And if you're going to make any accusation, I'd like some facts and proof to go along with it."

"She's a gold digger. What more proof do you need?"

"Something that'll hold up in court," Drury flatly answered.

"Something like phone records," Grayson added the moment he ended his call. Drury hadn't heard Grayson's conversation, but apparently he'd learned something. Judging from Jeremy's expression, it wasn't anything good, either.

Grayson turned to Drury. "SAPD examined Jeremy's phone records and discovered four calls from our missing kidnapper, Ronnie."

Yeah, definitely not good for Jeremy. "Want to explain those calls?" Drury demanded.

"I didn't know who he was, all right?" The volume of Jeremy's voice went up a notch. "He said he was interested in investing in one of my business ventures. I had no idea he was into anything illegal."

Maybe, but Drury wasn't going to take the man's word for it. "Did SAPD get anything else?" Drury asked Grayson.

"Only that Jeremy was uncooperative and unable to give any details whatsoever about the people he claimed kidnapped him."

"They wore ski masks!" Not only did his voice get louder, the muscles in his face had turned to iron.

Obviously, Jeremy had a temper, and he wasn't saying or doing a thing to convince Drury that he hadn't been the one to orchestrate this plan to ransom the baby and attack Caitlyn and him. Of course, Melanie and Helen were still on his suspect list, too, and the three were going to stay there until the person responsible was caught.

"Did you have anything to do with what went on at Conceptions Clinic?" Caitlyn asked Jeremy.

Jeremy threw his hands up in the air. "So, now you're accusing me of that, too?"

"Did you?" she pressed.

"Of course not." He spat out some more profanity. "From what I've heard, Grant could have a kid out there because of the mess at Conceptions. You really think I'd have any part in creating an heir?"

"No," Caitlyn agreed. "But you might have had a part in trying to make sure that heir didn't exist."

Jeremy's eyes narrowed. "I'm sick and tired of

you making me out to be the devil in all of this. Why don't you go after my mother?"

"You'd love that, wouldn't you? Because with your mother behind bars, you'd control the estate."

Jeremy shrugged, clearly not denying that.

Drury had seen and heard more than enough from this clown, and the timing was perfect because Gage came in through the back exit. "The car's ready," Gage said.

That was all Drury needed. Apparently Caitlyn, too, since they both got moving.

"That's it?" Jeremy called out to them. He tried to follow them, but one of the deputies blocked his path.

Drury ignored him. "Is someone else going with us?" he asked Gage.

Gage nodded. "Someone I found in the parking lot." He opened the door, and that's when Drury saw Lucas in the front seat.

"Worried about me?" Drury joked when Caitlyn and he got into the backseat. Gage took the wheel. The moment they were all buckled up, he took off, heading onto Main Street.

Lucas glanced at him. Then at Caitlyn. Even though there was no way Lucas could have known about that near kiss earlier, his brother could no doubt see that the attraction was still there.

"Yeah, I am worried about you," Lucas admitted, but he didn't spell out what that worry included. However, Drury figured Caitlyn was part of that concern.

Lucas took out a photo from his pocket and handed it to Drury. "Either of you recognize her?"

Caitlyn leaned closer to Drury to have a look. Drury studied it, too. A young woman in her early to midtwenties. Brunette hair and slight build.

Drury and Caitlyn shook their heads at the same time. "Who is she?" Caitlyn asked.

"Nicole Aston."

Drury repeated the name under his breath to see if it would trigger any kind of recollection, but it didn't. "Should we know her?"

Lucas flexed his eyebrows. "I think she might have been the surrogate."

That certainly got Drury's attention. Caitlyn's, too. "How do you know that?" she asked.

"I ran a search on recent female missing persons in the state and found out that Ms. Aston was a college student. According to her friends, she was a surrogate. And she disappeared a week ago."

Bingo.

Caitlyn studied the photo a moment longer before she handed it back to Lucas. "I don't think I've ever seen her before. But I doubt Conceptions or whoever's behind this would have wanted me to cross paths with the surrogate."

Lucas made a sound to indicate he agreed with

that. "I just thought maybe she would try to get in touch with you. Especially if she suspected anything illegal was going on at Conceptions. Of course, maybe the powers that be made sure she didn't get suspicious."

Even though this conversation was important, Drury continued to keep watch around them. So did Lucas and Gage. Now that they were out of town, it was a little easier since there weren't many buildings. Just some ranches and a lot of open farm road.

"Do Nicole's friends and family have any idea where she could be?" Caitlyn asked.

Lucas shook his head. "Both her parents are dead. No boyfriend. Her *friends* are pretty much just her classmates who said she kept to herself a lot."

Which might have explained why Conceptions would have wanted her for a surrogate. Still, there was another possibility. "Nicole could have given birth and then changed her mind about giving up the baby. She could be in hiding."

Lucas agreed fast enough that Drury knew that he had already considered it. "Her bank account hasn't been touched in a week, though. Prior to that, there were monthly deposits of fifteen hundred dollars. I've put a tracer on the deposits, but it was wired in, probably from an offshore account."

In other words, the tracer was a long shot.

It also meant someone had tried to cover their tracks. Most people who hired a surrogate didn't need to have their tracks covered like that.

Drury was so caught up in what Lucas had just told him that he hadn't realized some of the color had drained from Caitlyn's face. "Someone could have killed her to silence her."

Yeah. Drury decided not to confirm that out loud. Besides, Gage made a sound that had his attention shifting in that direction.

"What the hell?" Gage grumbled.

Drury followed his gaze and asked himself the same thing. There was something on the road just ahead.

Gage slammed on the brakes, and Lucas and Drury automatically drew their weapons. That's because they got a better look.

That *something* was a body.

CAITLYN DIDN'T GET a long look at the person in the middle of the road. Drury had pushed her down onto the seat. All three lawmen kept their guns ready, obviously bracing for some kind of attack.

But nothing happened.

"I'll call Grayson," Lucas volunteered, and a moment later she heard him doing that.

The car also started to move again. Slowly. Gage was no doubt trying to get even closer to see if the person was truly dead or if this was some kind of ruse. After everything that had happened in the past twenty-four hours, none of them was in a trusting sort of mood, and Drury's gaze was firing all around them. No doubt searching for anyone who might be lying in wait.

"Blood," Drury said under his breath. "Anyone recognize him?"

Caitlyn lifted her head, just long enough to have a look at the man. He was belly down on the pavement, his face turned toward the car, and while his eyes were open, they were lifeless. Fixed in a blank stare.

For a moment she thought it was Ronnie since the man had the same hair color and a similar build, but it wasn't him.

She also glanced around at their surroundings. There were no houses. No other vehicles, either. Just miles of flat pastures stretching out on each side of them. Thankfully, there were only a few trees, and the ones that were nearby weren't wide enough to hide a gunman.

"Grayson's sending an ambulance and some deputies," Lucas relayed when he finished his call. "He'll be here in less than ten minutes." He tipped his head to the body. "Anyone else thinking it'd be a really bad idea to go out there and make sure the guy's dead?"

"Agreed," Drury and Gage said in unison.

"As soon as the deputies arrive to secure the

scene, we're out of here," Drury told her. Then he turned back to Gage and Lucas. "Keep an eye on the ditches," he added.

Caitlyn's heart was already racing, and that certainly didn't help. Some of the ditches could be quite deep on the farm roads. Deep enough for someone to use to launch another attack.

The seconds crawled by, and it felt like an eternity. An eternity where Caitlyn had too much time to think, and her thoughts didn't go in a good place.

Oh, God.

"This could be a diversion so kidnappers can go after the baby," she blurted out.

None of them dismissed that, which only caused her to panic even more, and Drury took out his phone. "I'll call the ranch," he said.

Even though she was close to both Drury and his phone, Caitlyn couldn't hear what he said to the person who answered. That's because her heartbeat was crashing in her ears now, but she watched for any signs on Drury's face that he'd just gotten bad news.

More of the long moments crawled by before he finally said, "Everything's okay there. The place is on lockdown. Two of the deputies are with the baby, and the ranch hands are all armed."

Good. Of course, that didn't mean all those

measures wouldn't keep the kidnappers from trying to take her again.

"Someone's coming," Lucas said, getting their attention.

Caitlyn had another glimpse over the front seat, and she saw the red truck approaching from the opposite direction. It wasn't a new model, and it appeared to be scabbed with rust. It definitely didn't look like the sort of vehicle that their attackers would use. Plus, this road led to several ranches, so it could be someone just headed into town.

Lucas, Gage and Drury lifted their guns anyway.

The truck slowed as it neared the body and their car, but because of the angle of the sun and the tinted windshield, Caitlyn wasn't able to see who was inside. She especially wasn't able to see when Drury pushed her back down on the seat.

Not a second too soon, either.

She got just a glimpse of the passenger in the truck. He threw open the door and aimed an Uzi at them.

A hail of bullets slammed into the car.

The sound was deafening, and the front windshield was suddenly pocked with the shots. The glass held. For now. But this wasn't just ordinary gunfire. The rounds were spraying all over the car, and even though it was bullet resistant, that didn't mean the shots wouldn't eventually get through.

"Hold on!" Gage told them.

That was the only warning they got before he threw the car into Reverse and hit the accelerator. The tires squealed against the asphalt as he peeled away.

The shots didn't stop, though. The gunman continued to fire into the car, and it didn't sound as if he was getting farther away. Because he wasn't. She glanced out again and saw that the driver of the truck was coming after them. The shooter was leaning out the window to fire at them.

Gage cursed and sped up, but he was driving backward, and the shots had taken off his side mirror.

"Stay down," Drury warned her.

She did, but Caitlyn wished she had a weapon. Judging from the last glimpse she'd gotten of the truck, it was going fast, and if it was reinforced in some way, the driver could ram into them and send them into the ditch. If so, they'd be sitting ducks.

"Backup's on the way," Drury reminded her. Probably because she looked terrified. And she was.

But Caitlyn was also furious with the gunmen and with herself. Here, once again, she'd put Drury and his family in danger, and she still didn't know who was responsible for this.

Jeremy and Melanie both knew Drury and she had been at the sheriff's office, and it wasn't much of a stretch for them to figure out that they'd be heading to the ranch. Of course, Helen could have known that, too. Any of the three could have sent these thugs to try to kill them.

And there was no doubt that's exactly what they were trying to do.

This wasn't a kidnapping attempt. No. Those bullets were coming one right behind the other, each of them tearing into the car and windshield.

"Enough of this," Gage growled.

He hit the brakes, and for several heart-stopping moments, Caitlyn thought he was going to get out and make a stand. However, he backed the car into a narrow side road. In the same motion, he maneuvered the steering wheel to get them turned around. He darted out right in front of the truck. So close that it nearly collided with them.

Gage sped off.

"We'll lead them straight into backup," Drury said. He took out his phone, no doubt to let Grayson know. "We need to take them alive," he reminded the others.

Yes, because it was the fastest way for them to get answers.

"Hell," Drury mumbled.

She wasn't sure why he'd said that, but the shots suddenly stopped. Caitlyn followed his gaze, and he was looking back at the truck. She lifted her head just a fraction and peered over the seat to see that the truck was turning around.

Mercy.

They were going to try to get away.

She could only watch as the truck U-turned in the road. And that's when she got a look at the driver. It was someone she recognized.

Ronnie.

Chapter Nine

Drury figured he should be feeling some relief right about now. After all, he had Caitlyn safely back at the ranch, and other than the unmarked car being shot to pieces, there'd been no other damage.

Well, not to Caitlyn, him or his family.

But a man was dead. They didn't have an ID on the guy yet, but he'd almost certainly been murdered to get them to stop in the road so they could be gunned down. It was a high price to pay.

Caitlyn was paying a high price, too. She wasn't crying or falling apart. Not on the outside anyway. However, she had the baby in her arms and was rocking her as if that were the cure for everything. It had certainly soothed the baby. She was sacked out, and maybe just holding the little girl would soothe Caitlyn, too.

As much as she could be soothed considering she'd come close to dying.

"Grayson will question all of our suspects again," Drury reminded her. He was at the front window, volleying glances between Caitlyn and Lucas. His brother was outside the guesthouse and was pacing across the porch while he talked on the phone.

No doubt pushing to get any updates on the attack.

Drury was thankful for his help because he didn't exactly want to have those phone conversations in front of Caitlyn. Not with that shell-shocked glaze in her eyes.

"Ronnie," she said under her breath.

She didn't add any profanity, but Drury certainly had whenever the man's name came up. He'd never believed Ronnie's story that he was the baby's father and innocent in all of this, but the attack proved it. Ronnie had definitely been behind the wheel of that truck.

So, who'd hired him?

Drury checked his laptop to see if there'd been any breaks on finding a money trail. Breaks on anything else for that matter. But nothing.

"There's an APB out on Ronnie," Drury told her. "Everyone will be looking for him."

That wasn't a guarantee that they'd find him, but the APB was a start.

She nodded, and he thought the shell-shocked look got even worse. He also noticed that not all the rocking was actually rocking. Caitlyn was trembling. Probably feeling pretty unsteady, too, because she eased the baby into the carrier that was on the coffee table directly across from her.

Drury glanced out the window again. In addition to Lucas, two other armed ranch hands were out there. The front gate was locked, and the perimeter security system was on. That meant things were as safe as they could possibly be, so he left the window, went to the sofa and sank down beside her.

Caitlyn squeezed her eyes shut a moment. Groaned softly. And she eased against him, her head dropping onto his shoulder.

"I can still hear the gunshots," she said.

Yeah, so could he. He didn't want to tell her that she would hear them for the rest of her life. But she would. So would he. And he would remember that look of terror on her face.

There wasn't really a way to comfort her right now, so Drury just slipped his arm around her and hoped that helped. It seemed to do that. For a couple of long moments anyway. Until she lifted her head, and her eyes met his.

Any chance of comforting her vanished. A lot of things vanished. Like common sense because just like that, Drury felt the old attraction.

"I don't know how to stop this," she said. Her voice was a whisper, filled with her thin breath.

She wasn't talking about the danger now.

It would have been safer if she had been.

Before he could talk himself out of it or remember this was something he shouldn't be doing, Drury lowered his head and kissed her. There it was. That kick. He'd kissed her plenty of times, but he always felt it. As if this was something he'd never tasted before.

And wanted.

He hated that want. Hated the kick. Hell, in the moment he hated her and himself. But that didn't stop him from continuing the kiss.

This would have been a good time for Caitlyn to pull away from him and remind him just how much of a bad idea this was. She didn't. She moaned, a sound of pleasure, and she slipped her hand around the back of his neck to pull him even closer.

She succeeded.

The kiss deepened. So did the body-to-body contact, and her breasts landed against his chest. He felt another kick. Stronger than the first one, and even though he knew it would just keep getting stronger and stronger, he kept kissing her.

It didn't take long for things to rev up even more, and if Drury hadn't heard the sound, the heat might have taken over. But the sound was the front door opening, and that caused Caitlyn and

Drury to fly apart as if they'd been caught doing something wrong.

Which they had been.

Kissing Caitlyn not only complicated things, but once again he'd lost focus.

Drury reached for his gun, but it wasn't necessary. Lucas came in, and yes, he'd seen at least a portion of the kiss. Or maybe he'd just caught the guilty look on Drury's face.

Lucas spared them both a glance, but his attention settled on the baby. He went closer, looking down at her, and he brushed his fingers over her toes that were peeking out from her pink gown.

His brother was certainly a lot more comfortable with the baby than Drury was. With good reason. Lucas was a father himself to a two-month-old son, and he was raising him alone since the baby's mother was in a coma.

Bittersweet.

Much the way Drury felt about this baby. He'd been protecting Caitlyn and the little girl, so that created a bond between them. But the old wounds were still there. Always would be.

"Grayson got an ID on the dead guy," Lucas said, sitting on the coffee table next to the baby. "His name was Morgan Sotelo. A druggie with a long record. No known family or address."

Which was probably why he'd been killed. No one would have missed him. Drury doubted the guy was actually involved in the attacks, and that sickened Drury. He'd been killed so that Ronnie and his henchmen could kill again.

"Nothing on Ronnie?" Caitlyn asked.

Lucas shook his head. "But the dashcam on the car recorded the whole attack, so we might be able to get an ID on the shooter since he wasn't wearing a mask. Sometimes, an ID leads to an address and friends or neighbors who might rat out his location."

A location that wouldn't be easy to find because the snake had no doubt gone into hiding. Temporarily, anyway. If Ronnie and the thug got another chance to attack, they would.

"Why do they want me dead?" she asked. "And why do they want her after I paid them the ransom?"

Drury had been giving that a lot of thought, and it wasn't a theory Caitlyn would like hearing. "If Melanie's behind this, she could want you out of the way, and then she could sell the baby to Helen."

Caitlyn's forehead bunched up and she nodded. "And the same could be true for Jeremy. Neither one of them would care if they put the child in danger, either, but Helen… Why would she risk something like that?"

"Maybe she hadn't. That still doesn't mean I'm taking her off the suspect list, though. After all, the men who attacked us are low-life scum. Even if Helen gave them orders to keep the child safe, that doesn't mean they followed those orders."

There was also a fourth possibility. That the low-life scum had gone rogue and were trying to cash in on a much bigger chunk of the money. After all, if they killed Caitlyn, Helen would rightfully be granted custody, and they could possibly milk a huge ransom from Grant's mother.

The baby whimpered, snagging their attention, and even though she did that a lot, this time she didn't go right back to sleep.

"She probably needs to be changed." Caitlyn got to her feet and lifted her out of the carrier so she could head to the bedroom.

She gave Drury a glance, and even though she didn't say anything, he saw the fresh concern in her eyes. Not for the attack this time. But because Lucas had witnessed that kiss.

Lucas watched her leave, no doubt waiting to discuss a subject that Drury didn't want to discuss. However, his brother didn't start that unwanted discussion. He just sat there, staring at Drury. Waiting. This was a brother's game of chicken.

"What?" Drury finally snapped.

Lucas kept staring. "I didn't say anything."

"You don't have to speak to say something."

The corner of Lucas's mouth lifted for just a

second. The smile faded fast. "If you stay, you'll have to forgive her."

In the grand scheme of things, forgiving her would be the easy part. "Caitlyn told me right from the beginning that she didn't want to get involved with a lawman."

Lucas nodded. "Because of her dad." He paused. "Last I checked, you're still a lawman."

"Yeah. The badge didn't stop us from landing in bed four years ago."

"And it won't stop you now," Lucas reminded him. "But maybe the notion of a heart-stomping will. You really intend to go through that again?"

Now, here was why he wished he could avoid this discussion. Because the answer was obvious. He didn't want to go through that again. Coming on the coattails of losing Lily, it had nearly broken him. And that's why somehow, some way he had to stop it. That started with finding the sick jerk who was behind the attacks.

He stood, ready to head to his laptop and get to work. That would also cue his brother that it was not only the end of this chat but also that he should be getting back to whatever he was supposed to be doing. However, before Drury could even take a step, his phone buzzed.

Grayson again. Since this could be an important update on the case, Drury answered it on the first ring.

"The lab just called," Grayson greeted. And he paused. "They put a rush on the test and got the DNA results for the baby."

CAITLYN TOOK HER time changing the baby so that Lucas and Drury would be able to have the talk that she could tell Lucas was itching to have. Lucas was no doubt out there right now lecturing Drury about the kiss he'd witnessed.

She was lecturing herself about it, too.

Of course, it wouldn't help. For whatever reason, she seemed to be mindless whenever she got within twenty feet of Drury. Just the sight of him could break down the barriers she'd spent a lifetime building. The trick would be continuing to build them, and that wouldn't be easy to do as long as Drury and she were under the same roof.

There was a knock at the door. A second later it opened, and she saw Drury standing there.

"What happened?" she asked, getting to her feet. She left the baby lying on the center of the bed. "Did Lucas chew you out for kissing me?"

When Drury didn't jump to confirm or deny that, she knew that this wasn't about his brother but that there was some kind of new information about the case.

"The baby's DNA results are back," he said.

Caitlyn sucked in her breath so fast that she nearly choked. "This soon?"

He nodded. "The baby is yours and Grant's."

Even though Caitlyn didn't have any trouble hearing what Drury had said, his words just seemed to freeze there in her head. For several seconds anyway. Then the relief came.

Sweet heaven.

This was her daughter.

She wasn't Melanie's. Not Ronnie's, either. Her child.

Drury went closer, took her by the arm and had her sit. Good thing, too, because the emotions came flooding through her. So fast and hard. The shock, yes. But there was something much, much deeper.

The love.

Caitlyn had felt the love the instant she'd seen the baby, but it seemed much stronger now. And complete. She was the mother of a child she'd always wanted.

Even though the baby had gone back to sleep, Caitlyn scooped her up and kissed her. She woke up, fussing and squirming a little, but Caitlyn continued to hold her. This time, though, she looked at her through a mother's eyes.

Yes, the love was overwhelming.

"Are you okay?" Drury asked.

Caitlyn managed a nod. She was more than okay. For a couple of seconds anyway, and then she remembered the danger. That was suddenly overwhelming, too, now that she knew someone had not only created her baby, they wanted to steal her back.

Drury sank down on the edge of the bed next to her. Not so that he was touching her, though, but it was still close enough to get the baby's attention. The little girl opened her eyes, and she stared at him as if trying to figure out who he was. The corner of her mouth hitched up in a little smile.

Caitlyn had read enough of the baby books to know that the smile wasn't a real one, but it certainly felt real. It must have to Drury as well because he returned the smile before his attention went back to Caitlyn.

"Grayson is letting Child Protective Services know so they'll stop pursuing temporary custody," Drury explained.

Good. That was one less thing on her list of worries. "And what about Melanie?"

"Grayson will let her know, too. Since no one has contacted her with a ransom demand, I think it's safe to say that Grant and she don't have a child."

Caitlyn had to agree. "The more I think about it, Melanie's baby claim made even less sense. The only thing Grant and I had stored at Conceptions was the embryo. There wasn't any of his semen for them to create an embryo for Melanie."

Drury nodded, and since he didn't seem surprised, maybe he'd already considered that.

"What about the safe house?" she added. Because it suddenly seemed more critical than ever to get her out of harm's way.

"It's ready."

She immediately heard the *but* in his tone.

"After what happened on the road earlier, I'm not sure it's a good idea to take her off the ranch," Drury continued. "It's next to impossible to secure all the farm roads and ranch trails, but we've got security measures in place here at the ranch."

Even though it was hard to concentrate, Caitlyn went through the pros and cons of that. Yes. And as much as she hated to admit it, the ranch was the safer option. For now. However, staying didn't accomplish one thing—putting some distance between Drury and her.

But she had to put the baby first.

Drury must have understood because he didn't try to keep selling her on the idea of staying put. He did look at the baby again, though.

"You'll have to name her," he said.

Yes. Caitlyn had held off on doing that because in her mind it would have made it harder to give her up if the DNA test had proved this wasn't her child. Now that she was certain, she couldn't just keep calling her "the baby."

"I did a list a long time ago and wanted Elizabeth for a girl and Samuel for a boy." She looked down at the baby, as well. "But Elizabeth doesn't seem to fit her, does it?"

Drury lifted his shoulder, maybe trying to dismiss any part in this, but then he made a sound of agreement. "What was your second choice?"

"Caroline." It had been her grandmother's name.

He tested it out by repeating it a couple of times and nodded. It was silly to be happy over his approval, but she was.

"Caroline," she verified.

The moment seemed too intimate. Something that parents would do together. And they definitely weren't parents.

Drury must have sensed that as well because he eased away from her. "Too bad Grant died not knowing he would become a father."

Caitlyn figured she should just give a blanket agreement to that and end the discussion. But she didn't.

"Grant didn't actually want a child," she confessed. "I was the one who pushed him to go to Conceptions. He wasn't sold on the idea. In fact, he told me if I had a child that he or she would be just *my* child."

That brought Drury's gaze back to hers, and he cursed. "And you went through with the egg harvesting anyway?"

"I thought he'd change his mind." She paused, shook her head. "*Hoped* he would. And I reasoned that even if he didn't, I'd still have a child." Caitlyn gave a nervous laugh. Definitely not from humor. "Now you know just how desperate I was."

He stayed quiet a moment. "But you didn't stay desperate for long after you found out he was cheating on you."

"No," Caitlyn had to admit. "I decided it'd be better to have him completely out of my life. That included using the embryo at Conceptions. In fact, I was looking into adopting a child right before all of this happened."

This baby was a miracle for her. A miracle that she prayed she could keep safe.

Caitlyn heard the footsteps a few seconds before Lucas appeared in the doorway of the bedroom. At least this time Drury and she weren't in a lip-lock, but that still wasn't an approving look on Lucas's face. Except she thought maybe the look wasn't for her since Lucas was putting away his phone. He'd likely just finished another of the calls he'd been taking and making since they'd arrived at the guesthouse.

"The FBI found a money trail for Ronnie," Lucas explained. "Payments, big ones, that were wired to his account. The surrogate, Nicole Aston, was paid from the same account."

So, it was all connected. Not that Caitlyn had thought otherwise, but it was chilling to hear it spelled out like that. The same person responsible for arranging for her baby to be brought into the world had also arranged for Caitlyn to be killed.

Drury slowly got to his feet, his attention focused solely on his brother. "And did the FBI learn who owned that account?"

Lucas shook his head. "Not yet. It's offshore and buried under layers of false information. But that trail wasn't the only one they uncovered. The FBI found out who received the ransom money."

Caitlyn got to her feet, too. "Who?" she asked.

Lucas looked at Caitlyn. "You."

Chapter Ten

Drury hated every part of what was happening. Caitlyn being accused of orchestrating her baby's kidnapping. Having to take her to the sheriff's office to be questioned by an FBI agent. Having her out in the open again so someone could attack her. But Drury thought all those were a drop in the bucket compared with the final thing about this that he hated.

That Caitlyn was having to leave her daughter after learning the child was actually hers.

Of course, the baby was well protected with two deputies and the ranch hands, but this should be a time for her to savor an hour or two of getting to be with her child instead of being interrogated for something Drury knew she hadn't done.

And his faith in her innocence had nothing to do with the kiss or the attraction between them. This was common sense.

"We'll get this all straightened out," Drury

assured her the moment Lucas pulled to a stop in front of the sheriff's office.

Caitlyn looked at him, and he could see the weariness in her eyes. "I didn't do this," she said.

It wasn't necessary for her to tell him that. Drury knew. No way would she have intentionally put a child, any child, in danger.

As they'd done with their previous visit, the moment Lucas pulled to a stop in front of the sheriff's office, Drury got Caitlyn out of the car and inside. Away from the windows, too. And he immediately spotted someone he recognized.

"You know him?" Caitlyn asked.

"Yeah. FBI Agent Seth Calder."

Seth did his own introductions with Caitlyn. It didn't surprise Drury that they wouldn't want him or one of his cousins to do this interview with Caitlyn. No way could they be impartial, but at least the Bureau had someone whom Drury considered decent and fair.

"Good to see you again, Drury," Seth said before shifting his attention to Caitlyn. "Wish this were under different circumstances, though." He motioned for them to follow him to one of the interview rooms.

Both Grayson and Gage stayed back, following protocol, but it'd take a lot more than protocol to keep Drury out of the room. Thankfully, Seth didn't turn him away when he ushered Caitlyn down the hall.

When they passed in front of one of the other rooms, that's when Drury noticed it wasn't empty. Helen was in there, and she was having a whispered chat with a man who was probably her lawyer.

"Yes, she's here," Seth volunteered. "I'm interviewing her next. Then I'm bringing in Jeremy. He should already be on his way over."

Drury wouldn't have minded talking to Jeremy, but maybe they could dodge the man for Caitlyn's sake. Of course, there was no dodging Helen.

"I want to talk to you," Helen snarled when her attention landed on Caitlyn.

"It'll have to wait," Seth snarled right back.

Seth ushered Drury and Caitlyn into the other interview room. "Arrest Helen if she tries to come in here," Seth told Grayson.

Since Helen had already started to do just that, apparently ready to continue the confrontation, it was a timely order. It got the woman to stop even though she shot a glare at Caitlyn.

Drury glared back at her, and he closed the door behind him as he went into the room with Seth and Caitlyn.

"I'm innocent," Caitlyn said right off the bat.

"Someone is setting her up," Drury added.

Seth didn't refute either of those claims, and

once they were seated, he slid some papers toward her. It was a report on the money trail. The one that seemingly led straight to Caitlyn.

Her mouth tightened as she read it. "Why would I take money from Grant's estate to pay myself?"

"Trust me, I had to think long and hard to figure out some possibilities. Maybe so that Grant's family wouldn't try to challenge it, or despise you for having it?"

"They'll always despise me. And Grant's will was written so that they can't challenge it. The money is mine. *Was* mine," Caitlyn corrected. "I used almost all of it to pay for the ransom."

"The ransom that's in an offshore account with your name on it."

"I didn't know anything about that account," she insisted.

Again, Seth didn't dispute that, but he did pause a long time. "I believe you."

Caitlyn released her breath as if she'd been holding it a long time.

"Someone did this to try to get you in legal hot water," he went on. "Not just for this but for the baby itself. The agreement you signed at Conceptions was that neither you nor Grant could use the embryo you stored without the other's written permission."

She nodded. "I did that so he wouldn't be able

to use the embryos after we divorced. He wasn't especially thrilled with the notion of fatherhood, not then anyway, but I didn't know if he would change his mind years later."

Seth made a sound of agreement. "Someone in Grant's family could file a civil suit against you, though, if they could prove you took the embryo illegally."

Drury was about to say there was no proof for that, but maybe that's what the bank account was about. If Caitlyn had the money, then she would look guilty.

Well, maybe.

"Even if she had stolen the embryo," Drury said, "why go through with a fake kidnapping and ransom?"

"I'm sure a lawyer could argue that it was to gain sympathy. Or that maybe she has some kind of need for attention."

Caitlyn cursed. A rarity for her. "The only thing I need right now is for my daughter, Drury and his family to be safe."

Drury silently added Caitlyn's name to that list. He didn't want her daughter to be an orphan, and that was just one of the reasons he had to keep her alive.

"Someone else could have access to this bank account," Drury pointed out.

"Yes," Seth readily admitted. "Unfortunately,

if someone else did this, I can't tell who. That's where I need Caitlyn's help. The person who created this bank account had access to her personal info. Her Social Security number, for example. That's the password for the account."

"Either Grant's mother or brother could have gotten that," Caitlyn insisted. "For that matter, Melanie could have, too."

Another sound of agreement. "They made it too obvious, though. I mean, why would you open an offshore account using your own name and Social Security number? Yes, it was buried under dummy corporation accounts, but it didn't have nearly enough layers for someone who was genuinely trying to hide dirty money."

Now it was Drury who was breathing easier. He'd known all along that she was innocent, but it was good to hear a fellow agent spell it out. That, however, led him to something else.

"Why did you want to bring Caitlyn in if you knew it was a setup?" Drury asked Seth.

"Because of this." He passed another piece of paper their way. "I didn't want to get into this over the phone, but this was in the memo section of the account. Most people with legit accounts just type in things like what the payment was for. What do you think it is?"

Drury and Caitlyn looked at the paper together. It was the letters *N* and *A* and the word *Samuel*.

"'*N, A,*'" Drury read aloud. Since there wasn't a slash between the letters, it probably didn't mean *not applicable*. He went through all the info they'd collected during this investigation.

Bingo.

"Nicole Aston," Drury and Caitlyn said in unison.

"She's the woman we believe was the surrogate," Drury added to Seth.

Seth nodded. "And who's Samuel?"

Drury started to shake his head, and then he remembered something Caitlyn had told him. "You said if you had a son, you'd name him Samuel. Would Helen, Jeremy or Melanie have known that?"

She stayed quiet a moment, giving that some thought. "Maybe." And she paused again. "But it could be a place. Helen owns an apartment complex, and it's on Samuel Street in San Antonio. I remember because when I first told Grant about my name choice for a baby, he mentioned it."

"Nicole could be there," Drury quickly pointed out. "But if she is, the apartment's not in her name."

Seth was already taking out his phone, and he made a call to get someone to look for her. The moment he was done, he stood.

"You can watch through the observation mirror when I question Helen," Seth said. "For now,

I'd rather both of you stay back, but she's clearly got a temper. If she doesn't spill anything useful, I might try to spark that temper by bringing you in to confront her."

Caitlyn and Drury nodded. He wanted Helen to spill all. However, he hated that once again, Caitlyn was going to have to be put through something like this, especially coming on the heels of being accused of having set all of this up.

Drury took her to the observation room and moved her away from the door just in case Helen came barreling out of the interview with plans to confront Caitlyn again. He doubted, though, that Seth would let that happen. Seth wasn't the sort to let Helen ride roughshod over him.

"If the attackers end up killing me," Caitlyn said, "please don't let Helen get custody of the baby. I know it's a lot to ask," she quickly added. "But I don't have anyone else to turn to."

Yes, it was a lot to ask, but there was no way Drury would refuse. No way he'd let Helen get her hands on the baby.

"You wouldn't have to raise her yourself," Caitlyn went on. "Just make sure she has a good home."

That was it. Drury stopped the gloom and doom with a kiss. All in all, it was a stupid way to stop it, but he didn't want Caitlyn going on about being killed. Even if someone had already tried to do just that.

Drury had intended the kiss to be a quick peck, but it turned into something that fell more into the scalding-hot range. It left them both breathless, flustered and wanting more.

It also distracted them.

Seth's interrogation could turn up something critical, and here he was complicating the hell out of things by kissing Caitlyn again.

Drury forced his attention back on Helen, and he both heard and saw her deny whatever Seth had just asked. Her shoulders were stiff. Eyes, narrowed. And she was volleying glares between Seth and the observation window where she no doubt knew Caitlyn and Drury were watching.

"I didn't arrange to have my granddaughter born," Helen snapped. She jumped up and got right in Seth's face. "But I will be part of her life. A *big* part, without anyone interfering." That was obviously aimed at Caitlyn. "You won't stop that, and neither will my former daughter-in-law."

Seth had his own version of a glare going on, but it had a dangerous edge to it. "You should restrain your client before I do," Seth told her lawyer. His voice was edged with danger, as well.

And it worked. The lawyer took hold of Helen's arm and put her back in the seat. He whispered something to her, probably a reminder that it wouldn't help her case if she managed to get herself arrested.

"Tell me about your bank account in the Cayman Islands," Seth threw out there while he glanced through the papers he was holding.

Of course, there was no proof that it was indeed Helen's account, but the woman didn't know that. Well, if she was guilty, she didn't.

"I have no idea what you're talking about," Helen insisted, but before she could continue, her lawyer leaned in and whispered something else to her. "I have accounts in many places, so you'll have to be more specific."

"The account you used to orchestrate the birth of your granddaughter and the attacks on Caitlyn. You know which attacks I mean. The ones meant to kill her so she wouldn't be in your way." Seth leaned in closer. "On a scale of one to ten, just how upset are you that Caitlyn inherited all your son's money? I'm guessing a ten."

Judging from the way Helen's mouth tightened, she was about to deny the bank account and blast Seth for accusing her of attempted murder. However, Drury missed whatever she said because he heard the commotion in the squad room. Several people were shouting, and one of those people was Grayson.

"Put down the gun now," Grayson ordered.

That got Drury's heart pumping, and he automatically pushed Caitlyn behind him and drew his gun. "Wait here," he told her.

With his gun ready, Drury leaned out from the door, not sure what he would see. After all, who was stupid enough to come into a sheriff's office while brandishing a weapon? And the person did indeed have a gun.

Melanie.

She was in front of the reception desk. Not alone, either. She had a man directly in front of her.

Ronnie.

And Melanie had a gun pressed to his head.

"MELANIE," DRURY CALLED OUT.

Caitlyn didn't release the breath she'd been holding. Not yet anyway, but she'd braced herself for an attack. Of course, that would be exactly what this was, though it wasn't Melanie's style to do the dirty work herself.

"Gun down on the floor now," Grayson demanded.

Caitlyn peered out the door for just a glimpse, and she saw a lot in those couple of seconds. It appeared that Melanie had taken Ronnie captive.

Appeared.

But maybe this was the start of an attack after all.

"Be careful," Caitlyn warned Drury when

he stepped farther into the hall. He had his gun pointed in the direction where she'd seen Melanie.

"I can't," Melanie insisted. "This is a dangerous snake, and I don't want him to escape."

"We won't let that happen," Drury assured her and went even closer.

Caitlyn had no choice but to stand there and wait. Pray, too. Because if Melanie started shooting, she might try to take out Drury first.

There was a shuffling sound, followed by some profanity from Ronnie.

"This crazy idiot tried to kill me," Ronnie accused.

"Obviously Melanie didn't succeed," Drury answered, and judging from his footsteps, he went closer to assist Grayson in containing whatever the heck this was.

When Caitlyn glanced around the jamb again, she saw that Melanie had been disarmed and that Grayson was cuffing Ronnie. Good. But she still didn't breathe any easier, not with Helen on one side of the building and now Melanie on the other. Plus, according to what Seth had told them, Jeremy was on his way to the station.

Soon, all their suspects would be under the same roof along with the thug Ronnie, whom one of them had no doubt hired.

"I did your job for you," Melanie bragged. "I found Ronnie and brought him here."

"I'll want to hear a lot more to go along with that explanation," Drury insisted.

"She sneaked up on me and clubbed me on the head," Ronnie jumped to say. It was possible that had happened, but with Ronnie's other injuries from the car accident, it was hard to tell.

"Yes, I clubbed him," Melanie admitted. Her gaze shifted to Caitlyn when she stepped out of the interview room and into the hall. "Still think I'm behind this?" Melanie challenged.

Caitlyn shook her head. "I'm not sure what to think." And she didn't. This could all be some kind of ruse to make Melanie look innocent.

Or to distract them.

Obviously Drury felt the same way because he motioned for her to stay back.

"She had no right to club me like that," Ronnie protested.

No one in the squad room gave him a look of even marginal sympathy. "You're a fugitive," Grayson pointed out, "and you tried to commit murder."

"But I didn't." Ronnie didn't shout exactly, but it was close. "I've been framed. I didn't escape, either. I was dragged at gunpoint from the hospital."

Caitlyn had had enough. "You were in the same vehicle with the person who tried to kill us."

"Because he forced me to be there! Just like this bimbo."

Melanie didn't go after the man for the name-calling, but she shot him a glare that could have melted a glacier.

"I'm not saying another word until my lawyer gets here," Ronnie added.

Gage stepped forward and handed Grayson a piece of paper, and he took over with Ronnie. "I'll put him in a cell," Gage offered.

Grayson nodded, his attention on whatever was on that paper. He didn't turn back to Melanie until he'd finished it.

"Now, explain to me how you found Ronnie?" Grayson prompted the woman.

"I did your job," she snapped.

Drury went to stand by Grayson's side, and the pair just stared at her, waiting for her to continue.

"I had some PI friends looking for him," Melanie went on. "When they spotted him, they called me."

"And why didn't you call the police?" Grayson asked, sounding very much like the lawman that he was.

"Because you let him get away once, and I wasn't going to let that happen again. Make sure this time you keep him under lock and key. I don't want Ronnie out on the streets where he'll have a chance to kill me."

Drury and Caitlyn exchanged glances. "Why would Ronnie want you dead?" Caitlyn pressed.

Melanie threw her hands in the air. "I don't know. But someone's been following me, spying on me," she quickly added. "And what with the attacks, I figured Ronnie had his sights set on me next."

Caitlyn had to shake her head. "That doesn't make sense. There's no reason for Ronnie to want you dead."

"There is if Helen wants to silence me. She knows I'm not going to just let this drop. She stole from Conceptions Clinic to create a child Grant didn't want. He's not around to fight for what's right, so I'll do it for him."

Caitlyn huffed. "Didn't you try to do the same thing? Or else you claimed to do it."

Melanie pulled back her shoulders. "What do you mean—*claimed*?"

"I got the DNA results. The child is mine and Grant's. Not yours. Not Ronnie's, either. And with only one viable embryo, there's no way Conceptions could have used a surrogate to carry yours and Grant's child."

Melanie opened her mouth, closed it, then opened it again. She seemed genuinely stunned. "Those people at Conceptions duped me," she finally managed to say. But then in a flash the fire returned to her eyes. "Or you're lying. That's it, isn't it? You're lying and so is Helen. She wants me dead."

Caitlyn wasn't sure if the woman was plain delusional or truly believed Helen had a motive to kill her. Either way, Caitlyn didn't have time to press her on the issue because she saw a man making his way to the sheriff's office.

Jeremy.

Drury obviously believed this could be the start of another attack because he stepped in front of her again. "Go back to the observation room," he whispered to Caitlyn.

She hated that once again Drury might have to fight a battle for her, but Caitlyn didn't think this was the time to stand her ground. Especially since it could be a distraction for Drury and Grayson. She hurried back to the room but stayed in the doorway so she could watch what was happening.

"Are you the one who hired Ronnie to come after me?" Melanie asked Jeremy before he'd fully gotten inside.

He drew in a long breath, huffed and shifted his attention to Drury. "Has Melanie been telling you lies about me?"

"I'm not sure," Drury answered. "Did you hire Ronnie?"

Unlike his mother, he didn't have a flash of temper. Not on the outside anyway, but Caitlyn knew the anger was simmering just below the surface.

"No," Jeremy answered after several long moments. He reached into his pocket, prompting Grayson and Drury to go for their guns. "I'm just getting this." He pulled out a USB drive and handed it to Drury. "You'll want to go over what's on there."

"Why?" Drury asked. He passed it to one of the deputies.

"Because it's got everything you need to convict her of these crimes." Jeremy tipped his head to Melanie.

The woman howled out a protest, and she bolted forward as if she were about to rip the storage device from the deputy's hand. Drury blocked her path and turned toward Jeremy. "What's on there?"

"Lies," Melanie insisted.

"Transcripts of conversations that I had with Melanie."

This time Grayson had to physically restrain the woman. "You're a pig!" she shouted, the insult aimed at Jeremy.

Jeremy certainly didn't deny that. "Melanie and I had an affair. A short one," he emphasized. "I recorded our conversations, and in several of them, she says outright that she wants Caitlyn dead."

Melanie called him more names, punctuating it with plenty of ripe curse words. "You'll pay for this, Jeremy. Just wait. You'll pay."

It was hard to hear over Melanie's screeching,

and Grayson must have gotten fed up with it because he handed Melanie off to the deputy. "Put her in a holding cell until she calms down."

The deputy carried her away while Melanie shouted obscenities and threats.

"Do you always record conversations with your lovers?" Drury asked once the room was quiet again.

"Always." He tipped his head to the USB drive that the deputy had put on the table. "Somewhere around page thirty, Melanie says she wants to steal the embryo from Conceptions so she could use the baby to get Grant's money from Caitlyn."

Caitlyn's stomach twisted. Was that what this was really all about? A way for Grant's mistress to get his money?

"You said it was transcripts," Caitlyn said, going closer now. "Those can be easily faked. The only way we'd know if it was true would be to listen to what Melanie actually said."

"The recordings were accidentally erased." Jeremy waited until after both Grayson and Drury had finished groaning. "But Melanie mentions a bank account. Offshore. There could be something to help you identify where the account is and if it's the one used to pay off men like Ronnie."

Maybe it was the same account that Seth had found. Of course, maybe Jeremy was just doing this to take suspicion off himself. If so, it wasn't working. Jeremy would stay on her list of suspects.

"Go ahead." Jeremy tipped his head to the storage device. "Read what's on there."

Grayson shook his head. "It could contain a virus to corrupt our files. I'd rather have the FBI check it out. Plus, it could be a waste of my time. And if it is, if you're trying to manipulate this investigation, I can see if obstruction of justice charges apply here."

Judging from the way Jeremy pulled back his shoulders, he didn't like that one bit. Maybe this was an attempt to destroy some evidence by corrupting the computer system. If so, then Grayson would definitely have some charges to file against the man. Too bad those charges wouldn't put Jeremy in jail for long, though.

"Why would you sleep with Melanie?" Caitlyn asked him. "You knew what she was."

He lifted a shoulder. "I blame it on sibling rivalry. I never liked Grant having something I didn't."

It surprised her a little that he admitted it, but then Caitlyn remembered that Jeremy had once hit on her. She'd refused, and she had always thought that was one of the reasons he hated her so much. But maybe it was simply a case of him hating what he couldn't have.

"How did the recordings get *accidentally* erased?" Grayson asked.

Jeremy huffed. "Obviously I'm wasting my time here when I was just trying to do you a favor."

"A favor like Melanie bringing in Ronnie?" Drury didn't wait for an answer. "The only favor we need from either of you is concrete proof to stop these attacks. You got that kind of proof?"

"No," Jeremy said after a long pause and a glare. "But you have to consider that Caitlyn brought this on herself."

Caitlyn tried not to react to that, but she flinched anyway. The memories of the attacks were still too fresh in her mind. Always would be. "I didn't bring this on myself," she managed to say.

Jeremy made a *whatever* sound. "You knew what Grant was before you got involved with him."

It felt as if he'd slapped her. Because it was true.

Jeremy turned as if to leave, but Grayson stopped him. He motioned for a deputy to come closer. "Make sure Mr. Denson isn't armed and then take him to the interview room."

"What?" Jeremy howled. "You're still questioning me even after I bought you the dirt on Melanie?"

"Yes," Grayson said.

Despite Jeremy's protests, the deputy frisked him. No weapons so the deputy led him through the squad room and to the interview room directly across the hall from his mother.

"Jeremy's right," Caitlyn said under her breath. "I should have seen that Grant wasn't who he was pretending to be."

"He's not right," Drury snapped, and he slid his arm around her waist. "Everything Jeremy says and does could be to cover his tracks."

Caitlyn knew that, but it still didn't rid her of some guilt in this. If she'd never gotten involved with Grant, none of this would be happening.

"You wouldn't have your daughter if you hadn't been with him," Drury said as if reading her mind.

It was the perfect thing to say, and it eased some of the tension that had settled hard and cold in her chest. At least it eased it until she noticed that Grayson was looking at the paper that Gage had given him right before Jeremy had shown up.

"Bad news?" she asked.

Grayson didn't hesitate. He nodded. "SAPD sent someone to Samuel Street to find out if Nicole was staying there."

That got Caitlyn's attention. "Was she?"

Another nod. "The super ID'd her from a photo. The lease wasn't in her name but rather a corporation. One of the dummy companies on the offshore account."

That didn't surprise Caitlyn since Nicole—and Ronnie—had been paid from that same account.

"Nicole wasn't there," Grayson went on, and he handed the report to Drury. "The place had been ransacked, and there was some evidence of a struggle."

Oh, mercy.

"What kind of evidence?" Caitlyn pressed when Grayson didn't continue.

Grayson met her gaze. "Blood."

Chapter Eleven

Blood. Definitely not a good sign.

Especially this kind of blood.

According to the report Grayson had given Drury to read, SAPD had found high-velocity blood spatter on the wall of the living room in the apartment where Nicole had been staying. That meant there'd probably been some blunt-force trauma.

Reading that was enough to make the skin crawl on the back of his neck, but there was more. Much more. And that more was something Drury wasn't sure he wanted Caitlyn to know.

"They killed her," Caitlyn said.

That's when Drury realized the color had drained from her face. She also didn't look as if she could stand on her own, so Drury tightened his grip on her.

"We don't know for certain that Nicole's even dead," Drury insisted, and Grayson gave a variation of the same before he went to the cooler to get Caitlyn a drink of water.

"If they didn't kill her, that means they hurt her," Caitlyn amended.

"Not necessarily. It might not be her blood," Drury tried again, though that was reaching.

After all, the person who'd hired her to be a surrogate could want her murdered to tie up any loose ends. Nicole wouldn't be able to ID anyone if she was dead.

Caitlyn's hand was shaking when she took the paper cup of water from Grayson. Her voice shook, too, when she thanked him. That's when Drury knew he needed to get her out of the squad room. Away from the other officers. And especially away from the windows. After all, they had their three suspects under the same roof, and it was possible hired thugs were also nearby.

With the report still in his hand, Drury took her to the break room at the end of the hall, and he shut the door. With Helen and Jeremy just a few yards away, he didn't want Caitlyn to have another encounter with them. Not until she'd steadied her nerves anyway. As much as Drury hated it, sooner or later she'd cross paths not only with Helen and Jeremy but also with Melanie.

"I have to get back to the ranch," she said. "I need to see my baby."

Drury understood that, but the timing wasn't

good. "Grayson, Gage and the other deputies are tied up right now. Just hold on a little while longer until we've got someone to drive back with us."

She looked up at him. Nodded. But he could tell the only place she wanted to be right now was with her daughter.

And that would happen.

However, Drury kept going back to the idea that there were probably hired guns nearby, and he didn't want those guns taking shots at them. That meant clearing the area before he took Caitlyn from the building.

Caitlyn shook her head as if she might argue with that, but then the tears sprang to her eyes. "I'm so sorry about putting you in the middle of all of this trouble."

Drury wanted to snap at her for the apology. It was an insult to a lawman since the only reason he had a job was *because* of trouble. But considering he'd also kissed Caitlyn blind, it was a different kind of insult.

Of course, he shouldn't have been kissing her, either, so he wasn't exactly blameless in the insult department.

She looked at him, their gazes connecting, and even though he hadn't mentioned those kisses out loud, she was likely remembering them.

Feeling them, too.

Drury sure was.

The moment seemed to freeze or something. Well, they did anyway, but it didn't stop the old familiar heat from firing up inside him. Kissing her now would be the biggest mistake of all what with this emotion zinging between them, so he forced himself to look away, and his attention landed back on the report Grayson had given him.

It was several pages stapled together, and Drury made the mistake of flipping to the second page. To the picture that was there. Now the blood spatter was there for him to see.

And for Caitlyn to see, as well.

It'd been easy to sugarcoat the possibility of what had happened, but it was hard to sugarcoat something right in their faces. Along with the blood on the stark white wall, the coffee table and chairs had been tossed over. A lamp was on the floor.

So was a baby carrier. Next to the carrier was a diaper bag filled with supplies.

"Mercy," Caitlyn said, her voice filled with breath. "That's where she must have been holding Caroline."

"Maybe." But inside, Drury had to admit that the answer to that was *probably*. He only hoped the thugs had taken the baby to safety before they'd gone after the woman who'd given birth to her.

"Does the report say how long the blood had been there?" she asked.

Drury glanced through it, hoping that it was recent, as in the past hour or so. That way, it could mean the baby hadn't been around for whatever had gone on. Since there wasn't a body in the apartment, it could also mean that Nicole had escaped and was out there injured but alive. Or better yet, that she'd managed to bludgeon someone who'd tried to attack her.

But no.

"The CSIs will need to test it," Drury explained, "but it appears to have been there for several days." Maybe even as long as a week. That meshed with what her neighbors were saying—that they hadn't seen her in days.

Caitlyn blinked back tears, obviously processing what he was saying. It didn't process well. Because it meant the baby could have been there in the living room when the attack occurred. Caroline hadn't been hurt, but it sickened him to think that she could have been.

"Did anyone hear a disturbance in the apartment? Screams? Anything?" Caitlyn added.

"No." That didn't mean someone hadn't heard, though. The apartment wasn't in the best part of town. It was the kind of place where a lot of people would have turned a blind eye.

Caitlyn took the report from him, glancing

through it, and he saw the exact moment her attention landed on what he wasn't sure he wanted her to see. Her gaze skirted across the lines, gobbling up details that were probably giving her another slam of adrenaline.

"Nicole gave birth in the apartment," she said, her voice thin.

"The cops on the scene are only guessing about that." But it was a darn good guess considering the blood they'd found in the bedroom and adjoining bath.

There'd been evidence of a home delivery, including some kind of clamp that was used for umbilical cords. Other evidence, too, that Nicole hadn't been planning on staying put. They'd also found a plane ticket to California.

"She was taking the baby," Caitlyn whispered.

Everything was certainly pointing in that direction, especially since Nicole had already packed a diaper bag with baby supplies. Her wallet was missing, but Drury was betting she'd had enough cash to live on, for a while anyway.

"Nicole might have found out what was going on at Conceptions," Drury explained. "If she gave birth to the baby before her due date, she might have thought she could escape."

Of course, that meant the woman might have been trying to escape with Caitlyn's daughter, but Nicole might have believed this was the only way to keep the child safe. At least that's what Drury hoped she had in mind. There were cases of surrogates getting so attached to the babies they were carrying that they fled with the infants. No way, though, would the person behind this have allowed that to happen.

Not with a million-dollar ransom at stake.

Obviously, Caitlyn didn't have any trouble piecing together that theory, either, and because Drury thought they could both use it, he pulled her into his arms. She didn't resist even though they both knew this was only going to make things harder when this investigation was over. Still, with that reminder, Drury stayed put and probably would have upped the mistake by kissing her if there hadn't been a knock. Before Drury could untangle himself from her, the door opened.

Because every inch of him was still on high alert, Drury automatically reached for his gun again.

But it was just Grayson.

Like the other time he'd seen Drury close to Caitlyn, Grayson didn't react. He hitched his thumb in the direction of the interview rooms. "You'll want to come out for this," he said. "I think all hell's about to break loose."

"Not another attack?" Drury quickly asked.

Grayson shook his head and motioned for them to follow him. They did with Drury keeping Caitlyn behind him, and they stopped along with Grayson in the door of the interview room. Drury hadn't been sure what he would see once he looked inside. Jeremy was there as expected, but so was Helen, her lawyer and Melanie. It wasn't standard procedure to get suspects together for a joint interrogation, so Drury had no idea what was going on.

Seth was standing at the back of the room, his back against the wall, and he was eyeing their trio of suspects as if they were all rattlesnakes ready to strike.

"You're making a huge mistake," Jeremy said like a warning, and his comment was directed at Melanie.

Drury figured this was just a continuation of the verbal altercation they'd had in the reception area, but then he saw the photo on the phone screen in the center of the table.

"I don't even know why I'm in here," Helen grumbled. "I had nothing to do with that."

Drury went closer with Caitlyn following right behind him.

"That's Jeremy," Melanie announced.

Yes, it was, and the man was in some kind of waiting room. Drury looked at Grayson for an explanation, but Melanie continued before he could say anything.

"That's Jeremy at Conceptions. He was there to try to steal the embryo so he could destroy it."

Drury expected Jeremy to jump to deny that. He didn't.

"Tell them how you got those photos," Jeremy countered.

Melanie hiked up her chin. "I hired a PI to keep an eye on Conceptions. Because I was worried that someone would try to do something dirty. What I did isn't against the law."

"It's not against the law for Jeremy to have been there, either," Helen pointed out.

"Don't defend me," Jeremy snapped.

"I wasn't." Helen's voice was filled with just as much venom as her son's. "I was about to explain that Melanie could have hired that PI to steal the embryo, as well. But these pictures aren't proof that either of you committed a crime."

Everyone turned to the woman. Because that didn't sound like some kind of general statement. It sounded as if she had firsthand knowledge.

"You know something about this?" Grayson pressed.

"I don't know anything," she insisted, "but common sense tells me it didn't have to be Melanie or Jeremy who took the embryo. Caitlyn has a much stronger motive than either of them. And she couldn't have legally gotten her hands on them because she wouldn't have been able to get permission from Grant."

"That's true," Caitlyn admitted. "But I didn't steal them." She looked at Jeremy. "Did you?"

Jeremy took his time answering. "No." A muscle flickered in his jaw. "But I considered it. Briefly," he quickly added. "And I dismissed the idea just as fast. Frankly, I didn't think you'd want to have Grant's baby, not when you've obviously still got a thing for the cowboy here."

Caitlyn opened her mouth, probably to deny what Jeremy was saying, but since Drury and she had nearly just kissed again, she didn't voice her denial.

"So, if you thought I wouldn't want Grant's baby," Caitlyn continued a moment later, "then why consider stealing the embryo?"

Jeremy gave her a flat look. "You're not the only player in this sick game, Caitlyn. Mommy wants a grandbaby. I think she has hopes of getting it right this time, since she screwed up with Grant and me. But personally I'd like to make sure she doesn't get another chance at motherhood."

Jeremy sounded convincing enough. And maybe he was telling the truth. That didn't mean, though, that he hadn't created an heir to use as some kind of blackmail for his mother and Caitlyn.

"I did the best I could with the likes of you,"

Helen snapped. "You've always been an ungrateful son."

Jeremy faked a yawn. "Unstable mothers produce ungrateful sons. Am I done here?" he asked Grayson.

"No, he's not done!" Melanie howled. "You need to arrest him."

Grayson huffed. "And I'm sure Jeremy will claim I need to arrest you for what's on those transcripts." He looked at Helen. "You probably want me to arrest both of them."

"I do," Helen verified. "And Caitlyn. I know she had something to do with all of this."

Caitlyn went closer, practically getting right in the woman's face. "I would never do anything that would put my child in harm's way."

Helen stared at her a moment, then shifted her attention to Drury. "Are you the baby's father?"

Well, he sure hadn't seen that question coming. "No." Though he hated to dignify it with an answer.

Helen's stare turned to a glare. "I want to see the baby's DNA results."

"Get a court order," Drury tossed back at her. "If you can."

And he doubted she could since Caitlyn wasn't using the baby to make any kind of claim on Helen's estate. Of course, that wouldn't stop Helen from trying to get those visitation rights or even custody of the baby.

"Am I free to go?" Jeremy repeated.

Grayson didn't jump to answer. He made Jeremy wait several long moments. "Yeah, you can go. Not you two, though." He pointed first to Helen and then Melanie.

Obviously neither woman liked that. Both started to protest, and again Helen's lawyer had to restrain her. That's when Drury decided it was time to get Caitlyn out of there. Seth stepped up to take Helen and her lawyer back to the interview room across the hall. Grayson went in with Melanie, and he shut the door. Jeremy walked out the front of the sheriff's office without even sparing them a glance.

Drury kept his eyes on Jeremy until he was out of sight. "How deep do you think he's into this?"

Caitlyn shook her head. "I don't know, but I just hope they're not all working together."

Drury agreed, though he doubted they trusted each other enough for that, and he was certain there was plenty they weren't telling him.

"We can't leave yet, can we?" Caitlyn asked. He could hear the weariness in her voice and see it in her eyes.

Not with Grayson and the deputies still tied up, but maybe Drury could get some outside help. He took out his phone to call Lucas. Maybe his brother could arrange to bring a couple of the ranch hands with him. Drury definitely didn't want Caitlyn out of the building until he had some security measures in place. However, before Drury could even press his brother's number, he spotted Gage coming toward him. Fast.

"You've got a call through nine-one-one," Gage said, sounding a little out of breath. "The caller says she's Nicole Aston."

Chapter Twelve

Caitlyn tried not to get her hopes up, but that was impossible to do. After everything she'd just read in the report of Nicole's apartment, she had thought the surrogate was likely dead.

And she might be.

This call could be a hoax, designed to make the cops think a murder hadn't occurred. After all, it wasn't as if Drury or she would actually recognize Nicole's voice. Still, this was a thread of hope that didn't exist a couple of minutes ago.

She followed Drury to Gage's desk. The call had come in through the landline, and Gage put it on speaker.

"Nicole?" Drury asked. "I'm Agent Ryland. Where are you?"

"Is Caitlyn Denson with you?" the woman immediately said. Clearly, she was ignoring Drury's question.

"I'm here," Caitlyn answered. "Are you the surrogate who carried my daughter?"

"I am." A hoarse sob tore from her mouth. Too bad Caitlyn couldn't see the woman's face so she could try to figure out if she was faking that agony. "I swear I didn't know what was going on. Not until it was too late."

"Where are you?" Drury pressed.

"I can't say. Not yet. Not until I'm sure I can trust you."

"You can trust us," Drury assured her. "But the real question is—can we trust you?"

"Yes," she said without hesitation. "I had no part in anything that happened. Like I said, I didn't know what was going on until shortly before I gave birth."

"How did you find out what was *going on*?" Drury again.

This time there was some hesitation. Several long seconds of it. "I overheard some things, and I was able to piece together what was happening."

Drury huffed. "I'm going to need a lot more information than that. First, though, I have to make sure you're safe."

It sounded as if Nicole laughed, but it wasn't a laugh of humor. "I'm definitely not safe. Someone tried to kill me in my apartment."

"Yeah, I saw the photos. SAPD is there now. Is that your blood on the wall?"

"No. I hit one of the men who attacked me." Another pause. "God, I was just trying to protect the baby."

Hearing that robbed Caitlyn of her breath. Her daughter had been there with all that violence going on. Well, she had been if Nicole was telling the truth. Caitlyn had so many questions.

So many doubts, too.

"How do I know you're really the surrogate?" Caitlyn asked her.

More silence. "The baby I delivered had a small birthmark on her right ankle."

Bingo.

"She could be lying," Drury whispered to her. "She could have just seen the baby, that's all. Or could have been told about the birthmark."

Yes, and it didn't take Caitlyn long to realize why this woman would lie about something like that. She could be trying to gain their sympathy. Their trust. So she could use that connection to draw them out or find the location of the baby.

"How did you know the baby you were carrying was my daughter?" Caitlyn had so many more questions for the woman, but this might be the start to helping her understand the big picture of what had gone on at Conceptions.

"I knew something was wrong with the surrogacy arrangement," Nicole said. "Too much secrecy, and they were paying me in cash. Each month a man would show up with the money, and sometimes he would move me to a different place."

Yes, definitely secrecy.

"Then about two weeks ago I heard the man talking on the phone," Nicole went on, "and he mentioned your name. I did an internet search. Internet searches on Conceptions, too. All the mess that went on there."

There had indeed been a *mess*. Other babies born just like her own daughter, and all for the sake of collecting a huge ransom.

"Why are you calling exactly?" Drury came out and asked her. "Do you want me to arrange protection for you?"

"I want you to arrest the men who attacked me. Until they're caught, I'm not safe. None of us are safe."

That was the truth. Because even if Nicole was working for the person who'd orchestrated this, it didn't mean her boss would keep her alive. If the attack in her apartment was real, then Nicole would have realized she was a target.

"Give me some information so I can arrest them," Drury insisted.

Nicole sobbed again. "I can give you physical descriptions, but I don't know who they are, and they were both wearing ski masks."

"And they're the ones who took the baby?"

Caitlyn asked, though she wasn't sure she actually wanted to hear the answer.

"They did." Another sob. "I swear, I tried to stop them, but I knew if I stayed there and fought them, I'd lose. I'd just delivered the baby, and I was weak."

Drury and Caitlyn exchanged glances, and she saw the skepticism in his eyes. There were holes in what Nicole was telling them. Because if she was indeed so weak, how had she managed to fight off two hired guns.

"What about the blood in my apartment?" Nicole continued. "There must have been blood. Was there a DNA match?"

"Not yet. The CSIs haven't had time to do that. But they will."

"Good. Maybe that'll help you find them."

"You could help with that, too," Drury went on. "You need to tell me where you are so I can send someone to get you."

"No! I can't risk that. Those men could have tapped the phone lines."

"This line is secure," Drury assured her.

"Nothing is secure right now."

Caitlyn couldn't be certain, but it sounded as if the woman was crying. Maybe for a good reason—because it was indeed possible that nothing was secure.

"Nicole, you can't stay in hiding," Drury continued. "I can arrange protective custody for you with a team I trust. A team you can trust," he emphasized. "All you have to do is tell me where you are."

Silence. For a long time. "All right," Nicole finally said.

The relief Caitlyn felt faded as fast as it'd come when Nicole added, "But I'll do this under my own terms."

"What terms?" Drury snapped. "Because meeting you had better not involve Caitlyn going out in the open so someone can shoot at her again."

More silence from Nicole. "No. I won't involve Caitlyn. She's as much of a target as I am. Maybe more."

"How do you know that?" Caitlyn couldn't ask fast enough.

"I heard one of the thugs mention you by name. I heard a lot of things I shouldn't have," Nicole said in a whisper.

"What things?" Drury demanded.

"I'll tell you all about it when we're face-to-face. Let me find a meeting place. Once I'm sure I'm safe, I'll call you."

Drury groaned. "How long will it take you to set this up?"

"I'll need some time. It probably won't be until tomorrow. I'll call you when I have things in place."

Drury opened his mouth, no doubt to demand some of that info now, but Nicole had already hung up.

"Were you able to trace the call?" Drury immediately asked Gage.

"She was using a burner cell."

Drury cursed, and Caitlyn knew why. There was no way to trace a burner or disposable cell. Obviously, Nicole knew that. It could mean the woman truly was in danger, or it could all be part of a ruse to make them think that.

"You want me to assemble a protection detail?" Gage offered.

Drury shook his head. "I'll get Lucas to do it. You're already spread too thin here."

Gage didn't dispute that, and he stepped away when one of the other deputies motioned for him to go into the hall that led to the holding cells.

"I don't want you to have to wait around here any longer," Drury said, taking out his phone. He fired off a text. "Once Lucas gets here, he can escort us back to the ranch. You can stay there with Caroline while I meet with Nicole. If Nicole calls back, that is."

Yes, Caitlyn was skeptical, too. Even though the woman had reached out to them, it didn't mean she would cooperate.

"Nicole could be part of the dirty dealings that went on at Conceptions," Caitlyn threw out there.

Drury quickly agreed, and he led her back to the break room. Caitlyn was thankful to be away from Melanie and Helen, but she didn't like that troubled look in Drury's eyes.

"Nicole could have also called to pinpoint our location," Drury said.

Oh, mercy. Caitlyn hadn't even considered that.

"We'll just take some extra precautions," he assured her. But she must not have looked very assured because Drury hooked his arm around her waist and led her to the sofa. "I asked Lucas to bring a couple of the ranch hands with him."

"But you'll all still be in danger," she quickly pointed out.

He made another sound of agreement. "It might not be any safer to stay put."

Drury was right. Yes, this was the sheriff's office, but there'd been attacks here before, and the office was right on Main Street, sandwiched between other buildings and businesses.

"Are we safe anywhere?" she asked, but then Caitlyn waved off her question. She already knew the answer. They weren't.

The only silver lining was that, whoever was behind this, they seemed to be after her and not the baby. For now anyway. That could change if and when she was out of the way.

Caitlyn hadn't realized just how close Drury and she were sitting until she turned to look at him again. Too close. Practically mouth to mouth. She glanced away but not before she saw something else in his eyes. Not just worry and concern.

But the attraction, too.

And maybe even something else. Because his forehead was bunched up.

"Are you okay?" she asked, automatically slipping her hand over his.

"I've been having flashbacks," he finally said.

That wasn't what Caitlyn had expected him to say, but she should have. Of course, this would have triggered the horrific memories of his wife's death.

"The sooner you can distance yourself from me, the better," Caitlyn reminded him.

A new emotion went through his eyes. Anger, maybe, but it didn't seem to be directed at her. Judging from the way he groaned, he was aiming it at himself.

"Lily died right in front of me." His voice was a ragged whisper. "Did you know that?"

She nodded and hated that her own flashbacks came. She had seen a man die. Her father. And those were images she'd never forget. It had to be even harder for Drury because Lily had been pregnant. He'd lost his wife and baby with one bullet from a robber's gun.

"Yeah," he grumbled as if he knew exactly

what she was thinking. "We've both got plenty of emotional baggage."

They did, and that seemed to be a caution to remind her that neither of them were emotionally ready to have a relationship. And they weren't. That's why she was so surprised when his mouth came to hers.

There it was. That instant slam of heat. The one that could chase away the flashbacks. But that heat could also cloud her mind and body. Definitely not something she needed right now, but Caitlyn didn't stop him. Nor did she stop Drury when he upped the contact and deepened the kiss.

He slipped his arm around the back of her neck, easing her closer and closer. She didn't resist. Couldn't. Drury certainly wasn't the first man she'd ever kissed, but no man had ever drawn her in the way he did.

Caitlyn slid her arm around him, making the contact complete when her breasts landed against his chest. Now she got memories of a different kind. No flashbacks of violence but rather of the times they'd been together.

In bed.

Like his kisses, Drury had her number when it came to sex. She doubted that had changed, but she didn't want this need she felt for him. Didn't want the ache to build inside her. It complicated things and would only lead to a broken heart.

That didn't stop her, though.

She melted into the kiss. Melted into Drury until they were pressed against each other. Until the fire sent them in search of something *more*. And more wasn't something they could have. Not right now anyway.

Drury pulled back, and as if starved for air, he gulped in a deep breath before going right back to her again. This kiss wasn't as deep, but she could still feel the emotion. Could still sense the fierce battle going on inside him.

"I should regret that," he said with his lips still against hers. "I want to regret it," he amended.

"Same here." But she didn't, and judging from the way he groaned, neither did he.

"The baby," he added a moment later.

Caitlyn braced herself for Drury to tell her that he couldn't get involved with her because of the baby. Because Caroline would always trigger memories of his own child that he'd lost. Plus, Caroline would always be Grant's daughter, which would give Drury another dose of memories that he didn't want.

But he didn't get a chance to add more because Grayson opened the door.

"A problem?" Drury immediately asked, and he got to his feet.

"Possibly a solution. Ronnie just said he wants

to cut a deal. Information in exchange for reduced charges."

Of all the things that Caitlyn had thought the sheriff might say, that wasn't one of them. "Why the change of heart?"

Grayson lifted his shoulder. "Maybe he thought his thug cronies wouldn't be able to break him out of jail as easily as they got him out of the hospital."

True, but she was still suspicious, and she definitely didn't like the idea of a man who'd tried to kill them getting a lighter sentence. She wanted him behind bars for a long time.

"What's he offering?" Drury wanted to know.

"The name of the person who hired him."

There it was. Probably the only thing Ronnie could have put on the table that would have made this impossible to turn down.

"Of course, we can't begin to start working out a deal like that until his lawyer gets here," Grayson went on. "And the DA will have to be the one who approves it." He paused. "It could still fall through."

And it could take time. In fact, Ronnie could drag this out so long that there could be another attack. And this time, it might succeed in killing them.

Drury's phone dinged to indicate he had a text message. "It's Lucas," he said, glancing at the screen. "He's just out the back door with Kade. Two ranch hands are behind them in a truck."

Kade was another Ryland cousin. An FBI agent, and while Caitlyn was glad about having three lawmen for protection, that meant less security at the ranch.

"We can hurry," Drury told her as if he knew exactly what her concern was. He stood, helping her to her feet.

"I'll call you with any updates," Grayson assured them while he punched in the security code to disarm the alarm on the back door.

Drury thanked him and got her moving. Of course, he was in front of her and had his gun drawn when he cracked open the door and looked out. Lucas was indeed there, behind the wheel of what appeared to be an unmarked car. Caitlyn hoped it was bulletproof.

"Move fast," Drury reminded her.

He took a single step forward and then stopped cold. For a second anyway. Then he moved them to the side and peered out around the jamb.

Caitlyn couldn't see what had caused him to do that, but Lucas reacted, as well. He, too, drew his gun, and their attention shifted to the park area just behind the sheriff's office. There were clusters of trees and trails back there. Plenty of places for someone to hide, too.

"What's wrong?" Grayson also pulled his gun and joined Drury at the door.

"Someone's out there," Drury said.

Those three words caused Caitlyn's heart to slam against her chest. Please, no. Not another attack.

There were security lights on the back of the sheriff's office. Lights on the trails as well, but there wasn't enough illumination to see the whole area. Even though it wasn't pitch-dark yet because the sun was still setting, it would be easy for an attacker to use that dimness to his advantage.

"Don't shoot," someone called out.

A woman. And it was a voice that Caitlyn thought she recognized.

Nicole.

Chapter Thirteen

Hell. This was not how Drury wanted this to play out. He'd wanted to get Caitlyn out of there before something bad happened. And maybe this wasn't bad, but since it was unexpected, it had the potential to take a nasty turn.

Drury glanced at Caitlyn to make sure she was okay. She wasn't. Her breathing was already way too fast, and it was obvious she was getting another slam of adrenaline. His body was also gearing up for a fight.

A fight that he hoped wouldn't be necessary.

"Please don't shoot," the woman repeated. That voice sure sounded like Nicole's, but that call could have come from someone pretending to be the surrogate.

"Step out so I can get a good look at you," Drury demanded. "And put your hands in the air."

Even though she was probably a good twenty

feet away, he could still hear her gasp. "I'm not armed."

"Then prove it. Put your hands in the air." Drury didn't bother to tone down his lawman's voice. Better to be safe than sorry, and he wanted to make it clear to this woman that he would shoot her if she tried to attack them.

"Tell the other men to go away," Nicole bargained. "I don't trust them. And I want to see Caitlyn."

"That's not going to happen," Drury assured her. "Not until I know you're who you say you are. Step out now."

Drury wasn't sure she would. Not with four lawmen's guns trained on her. He figured the ranch hands in the truck behind the car had their weapons drawn, too.

"I don't want to die," Nicole said, her words punctuated with sobs.

"Then come out so I can help you," Drury offered. "You can come inside, and we'll put you in protective custody."

"No. That man is in there."

Drury had to think about that for a few seconds. "You mean Ronnie?"

"Yes."

He waited for Nicole to add more to that, and when she didn't, he asked, "How do you know Ronnie?"

A few seconds crawled by. "He's the one who

moved me into the apartment. He works for the people behind all of this, and if he gets the chance, he'll kill me."

Drury had no doubts about that. Well, no doubts if Nicole was telling the truth that is. But she didn't mention Ronnie in their other conversation. Only the two thugs who'd attacked her after she delivered the baby.

"I need to see your face," Drury tried again. "I need to make sure you're really Nicole Aston."

Just as when she was on the phone, there was a long silence. So long that Drury thought the woman might turn and run. He hoped that didn't happen because it could be part of a ruse to divide and conquer. Because at least two of them would have to go after her since she could have critical information to spare Caitlyn from yet another attack.

Just when Drury was about to give up, there was some movement. Not from the trees but rather from some shrubs.

"Stay back," Drury reminded Caitlyn. He wished there was time to move her to another part of the building, but he didn't want her out of his sight. Besides, there could be gunmen at the front of the building by now.

More movement in the shrubs, and finally the woman lifted her head. Not her hands, though.

"I want to make sure you aren't armed," Drury ordered.

She lifted her hands, slowly. No gun. Not one that was visible anyway, but that didn't mean she didn't have one nearby.

Drury picked through the dim light to study the woman's features. She looked like the Nicole Aston in the driver's license photo.

"I told you I wasn't carrying a weapon," Nicole said. "I came to you for help, but if you don't trust me, I'll have to go elsewhere."

"Someone's trying to kill Caitlyn. Maybe trying to take the baby, too. I have to be suspicious of everyone who might be connected to Conceptions."

And Nicole was definitely connected. The question was, just how deep was her involvement?

"Come in so we can talk," Drury tried again.

No hesitation from her that time. She quickly shook her head. "I want to see Caitlyn."

"I can't risk that," Drury said at the same time Caitlyn said, "I'm here."

Drury shot her a glare. He hadn't wanted Nicole to know Caitlyn's position, but then it was highly likely that Nicole had caught a glimpse of her the moment Drury opened the door.

"You need to do as Drury says," Caitlyn called out to the woman. "Come inside. It's not safe out there."

"I know," Nicole answered.

Apparently, she meant that because her gaze

was firing all around them. She appeared to be as much on edge as the rest of them because Lucas, Kade and Grayson were doing the same thing. Drury was trying to do that while keeping watch on Nicole. He still wasn't convinced that she wasn't about to pull out a gun.

Tired of this standoff, Drury decided to put an end to it. "Tell me what you came here to say, or else I'm shutting this door."

"I don't want to go to jail," Nicole said.

Once again, she'd surprised him. "For what?"

"I signed a lot of papers when I became a surrogate. A couple of months ago when I heard on the news about what had gone on at Conceptions, I got worried."

She was right to have worried. There'd been a lot of illegal things going on at the clinic.

"When Ronnie came by to give me my monthly payment," she continued, "I told him I wanted out of the deal. I was afraid what they might do to the baby. He said the papers I signed were like a confession. That if I went to the cops that they could use those papers to put me in jail. But I swear, I didn't have anything to do with stealing any embryo."

"I'll want to take a look at those papers," Drury insisted.

She shook her head. "The men who attacked me took them."

Maybe just more tying up of loose ends, but they also might have taken them because they could implicate their boss.

"That's why I need to talk to Caitlyn," Nicole went on. "Ronnie said the baby's mother could be arrested, too, because she's the one who helped with the plan."

"I didn't," Caitlyn quickly said. "I had no idea what was going on until I got the ransom demand."

"So, Ronnie lied."

Nicole's voice was so soft that Drury barely heard her. But there was something in her tone. Something in the way she said Ronnie's name. Maybe it was nothing, but it seemed as if Nicole might know more about him than she was admitting. Drury really needed to sit her down for an interview. There was no telling what she would reveal when questioned.

"Come inside," Drury pressed. "Caitlyn is in here, and the two of you can talk."

Nicole was shaking her head. Until he added the last part. Obviously, Nicole was very interested in seeing Caitlyn because she stopped shaking her head and made another of those nervous glances around her.

"All right," Nicole finally agreed. "But don't point your gun at me when I come out. I have panic attacks, and I don't want to trigger one."

A panic attack seemed the least of her concerns right now, but Drury glanced at Grayson. Grayson understood exactly what Drury wanted him to do because he stepped to the side, out of Nicole's line of sight.

And he kept his gun ready.

Drury lowered his to his side.

Even though Kade and Lucas were still armed, that didn't seem to bother Nicole. Perhaps because they were inside the car. Or maybe she wasn't able to see through the tinted glass. Either way, she pushed the shrubs aside and started toward them.

She didn't get far.

Nicole made it only a couple of steps before the shot blasted through the air.

THE SOUND OF the shot was so loud and seemed so close that Caitlyn thought for a moment that Drury had been shot. She caught onto him, pulling him out of the doorway, but he was already headed her direction.

Grayson scrambled to the other side.

It wasn't a second too soon because the next shot slammed into the jamb only inches from where they'd both been standing.

Outside, Caitlyn heard a scream. Nicole. Mercy, had the woman been shot?

Even though she wasn't certain she could trust Nicole and that she'd told them the truth about everything, Caitlyn didn't want her hurt. Or worse. Someone could be murdering her right now in front of them.

She fought the flashbacks of her own father's murder. Fought the fear, too, but that was hard to do. The adrenaline was already sky-high, and her heartbeat was crashing in her ears, making it hard to hear. Hard to hear Nicole anyway.

Caitlyn had no trouble hearing the next shot.

It, too, slammed into the doorjamb.

Drury cursed, pulled her to the floor and covered her body with his. Protecting her. Again. She wished she had a gun or some kind of weapon so she could help him, and while she was wishing, she added for the shots to stop.

They didn't.

Two more slammed into the building.

"Can you see the shooter?" Grayson asked Drury.

Drury shook his head. "But I think he's in one of the trees in the park. Somewhere around your ten o'clock."

That didn't help steady her nerves. Because that meant the shooter was in a position to keep firing. Which he did.

"What about Lucas and Kade?" Caitlyn had gotten only a glimpse of them before Drury had pulled her away.

"Still in the car. They won't be able to get out."

No. Because they'd be gunned down. That also meant they would have a hard time returning fire. But at least they were safe. However, she knew that shots could get through a bullet-resistant car.

"What about Nicole?" Caitlyn managed to say.

Another headshake from Drury. "I can't see her, either. I hope to hell she stays down."

Maybe that meant Nicole was still alive. Of course, she wouldn't be for long if they couldn't get her out of the path of the shooter.

Except the gunman wasn't firing at her.

"All the shots are coming into the building," Caitlyn said under her breath.

"Yeah," Drury verified. "It could mean Nicole's in on this. Or…"

He didn't finish that because another shot came at them. One that caused Drury to curse again. And she knew why. Because the angle of the shot had changed. Either the gunman had moved or there were two shooters.

Drury reached up, slapped off the lights and moved her even farther away from the door. Two deputies came in from the squad room, but Grayson motioned for them to get back. Good thing, too, because the shots went in their direction. Clearly, the shooter was pinpointing their moves, and with the lights off it could mean he was using some kind of infrared device.

"The walls and windows of the sheriff's office

are all reinforced," Drury said to her. Perhaps he gave her that reminder because she was trembling now and cursing as well with each new shot.

Caitlyn wasn't sure how many rounds were fired, but it seemed to last an eternity. And then it stopped.

Silence.

That was more unnerving than the shots because she knew it could mean the gunmen were closing in on them.

"Stay down," Drury warned her.

He reached in the slide holster of his jeans and handed her his backup weapon. Caitlyn took it, but she had no idea what he had in mind. Not until he started to inch away from her.

Toward the door.

She wanted to pull him back, to try to keep him out of harm's way, but there was no safe place in the room right now. Because if those gunmen got closer, they could start picking them off.

Grayson moved, as well. Both Drury and he stayed low on the floor, but they made their way to the door. Drury lifted his head, listening, and his gaze was firing all around the area. She suspected Kade and Lucas were doing the same thing.

"You can't let them take me," Nicole called out.

Caitlyn had no trouble hearing the terror in the woman's voice, and she instinctively moved to help her. She didn't move far, though, because Drury motioned for her to stay down.

"It could be a trap," he whispered.

She almost hoped it was. Because a trap like that would fail, and it would mean Nicole wasn't out there with hired killers. Of course, if it was a trap, it meant they had a very dangerous woman on their hands.

After long moments of silence, the sound of the next gunshot caused Caitlyn to gasp. And it didn't stay a single gunshot.

"I see him," Drury said to Grayson a split second before he leaned out and fired.

Caitlyn hadn't thought the shots could get any more deafening, but she'd been wrong. Because Grayson began to fire, as well. And the shooters outside didn't stop. However, even with all the noise, Caitlyn heard Nicole scream.

"No!" she shouted. "Please, no."

Mercy, did that mean she'd been hit?

Caitlyn lifted her head just a fraction so she could peer out the door, but the angle was wrong for her to see Nicole.

However, she saw something else.

She got just a glimpse of a man wearing dark clothes and a ski mask. Obviously one of the shooters. He took aim at Drury.

"Watch out!" Caitlyn warned him.

But no warning was necessary. Drury had already seen the man, and he fired two shots, both of them slamming into the shooter's chest. He made a sharp sound of pain and dropped to the ground.

"I think he's wearing Kevlar," Drury said to Grayson.

If so, then the guy might not be dead after all. He could just have gotten the wind knocked out of him, and once he regained his breath, he could try to kill them again.

"You see the other gunman?" Grayson asked.

"No."

Caitlyn figured it was too much to hope that he'd run away. And she soon got confirmation that he hadn't.

"Hell, he's going after Nicole," Drury spat out.

He scrambled to an even closer position by the door, and he took aim, but Drury didn't fire. Neither did Grayson nor the deputies.

"Please, no," Nicole repeated. Caitlyn hadn't thought it possible, but the woman sounded even more terrified than before.

"You want her dead?" someone called out. It was a man, but Caitlyn didn't recognize his voice.

"I want you to let her go," Drury answered.

"No can do. But if you shoot now, the bullet will go into her. Is that a risk you want to take?"

That meant this thug was using Nicole as a

human shield, and Caitlyn got a glimpse of that when the gunman moved into her line of sight.

Yes, he had Nicole all right.

The man had his left arm hooked around Nicole's neck. His gun was pressed to her head. And he was backing away from the building. Caitlyn also saw something else.

Another gunman.

The second guy was to the thug's right, and he had a rifle aimed at Drury and the others.

As terrifying as that was, this could also be a different kind of terror for Drury. Because this was almost identical to the way his wife had been murdered.

"What will it take for you to let her go?" Drury tried to bargain with the man. "She's innocent in all of this."

"I don't care. Just following orders, Agent Ryland. You really don't want to watch another woman die, do you?"

So the gunman knew who Drury was. And he knew about Drury's past. Not exactly a surprise, but she had to wonder why the gunmen had made such a bold attack. Plain and simple, it was risky because they'd fired those shots into a building filled with lawmen.

"Why do you want Nicole?" Caitlyn shouted.

That earned her another glare from Drury. Probably because he didn't want the gunman's attention on her and also because he figured the gunman wouldn't answer.

But he did.

"Nicole'll get a chance to tell you all about that," he said. "We'll be in touch soon."

"Don't let him take me!" Nicole shouted.

However, they had no choice but to let the gunman do just that. With his gun still against her head and with his armed partner leading the way, the man took off running, dragging Nicole with him.

Chapter Fourteen

We'll be in touch soon.

The gunman's words kept playing in Drury's head. The words of a kidnapper, not a hired killer. At least it didn't seem as if the guy had plans to kill Nicole. Not yet anyway.

But what did the gunman and his boss hope to gain from this?

Money was the obvious answer. Maybe since they didn't get an additional ransom from Caitlyn, this was a way of making up for that. Of course, this could be some kind of sick bargaining plan to get Caitlyn out in the open.

That wasn't going to happen.

She'd already come too close to being killed, and Drury had to put a stop to it. He also had to put a stop to the other images that kept going through his head.

Yeah, the flashbacks had come at the worst possible moment.

Thank God he hadn't frozen, but that's because he'd had to fight those old images by reminding himself that other lives were at stake. He couldn't go back in time and save Lily.

Hell, he hadn't saved Nicole, either, because the surrogate was in the hands of hired killers.

Drury nearly jumped when he felt the soft touch on his arm. He'd been in such deep thought what with wrestling his demons that he hadn't heard Caitlyn walk up behind him in Grayson's office.

"I wish it were something stronger," she said when she handed him a bottle of water.

Yeah, they both could have probably used something stronger, but it would have to do. Especially since they couldn't go anywhere. The break room was closed off, now essentially a crime scene, and the building was on lockdown until Lucas and the other deputies made sure the area was clear.

"I called the ranch," she added, "and talked to the nanny who's staying with Caroline. Everything seems to be okay there."

By *okay* she meant *safe*, but it wasn't truly okay because Caitlyn wanted to be there with her daughter. At least Caroline was in good hands. There were several nannies at the ranch, including this nanny, Tillie Palmer, along with plenty of cousins to help take care of her.

"We shouldn't have to be here much longer,"

he told her. Hoped that was true. And because he thought it would help, he brushed a kiss on her cheek.

It didn't help.

That look was still in her eyes. The look of a woman who'd just been through hell and back. Hell that wasn't over now that Nicole was a hostage and two of the gunmen had escaped.

The third was dying.

At least that was what the medic said when they'd whisked him away in an ambulance. The guy hadn't been wearing Kevlar after all, and both of the bullets Drury fired had gone into the man's chest. He was in surgery, but it wasn't looking good.

"Your family has really stepped up to help me," she said. "I won't forget that."

Yes, they had stepped up, and Drury wouldn't forget it, either. He, his brothers and cousins had a strong bond, and they didn't forgive easily when one of them was wronged. In their minds, Caitlyn had wronged him, but that hadn't stopped them from doing the right thing.

"You two okay?" Grayson asked from the doorway. He had his hands bracketed on the jamb.

Both Caitlyn and Drury settled for nods. Of course, they were lying, but at least they were alive, and none of his cousins or the other deputies had been hurt in this latest attack. It could have been much, much worse. It sickened Drury to think that Caroline could have been with them.

"Helen and Melanie are still whining about leaving," Grayson went on. "If they keep annoying me, I just might let them."

Of course, if it was one of them who'd hired the gunmen, then that person would be safe. The other could be toast.

"Any news?" Drury asked.

"Nothing on the wounded shooter or Nicole, but Gage just loaded the security footage." Grayson tipped his head to the laptop on his desk. "Kade's going through it, too, but it wouldn't hurt to have another pair of eyes on it."

Drury welcomed the task. Anything to get his mind off the flashbacks and that haunting look in Caitlyn's eyes. She must have welcomed it, too, because she joined him at the desk. Not exactly a good idea, though.

"You don't have to see this," he reminded her.

She dragged in a deep breath. "I have to do something."

He understood. Standing around with too much time to think was the worst way to deal with raw nerves. That said, he didn't want her to watch the actual shooting. Hell, he wasn't sure he wanted to watch that part, either.

Grayson left them, probably to go another round with Helen and Melanie, and Drury had

Caitlyn sit at the desk. He stood behind her and pressed the keys to load the security footage. There were four cameras, one on each side of the building, and the screen had the feed from all four. Drury focused on the one at the back.

He fast-forwarded through the footage, not really seeing much until Lucas and Kade pulled to a stop next to the rear exit. No sign of Nicole or the gunmen, though, so he froze the frame and zoomed in on the area where he'd shot the man.

Still nothing.

It took a few more tries before he finally spotted the gunman in the tree. He was well hidden behind a thick live oak branch, and it didn't help that his dark clothes and ski mask camouflaged him.

"I only see the one gunman," Caitlyn said. "You?"

He was about to agree, but then Drury saw the slight movement on the camera that faced the parking lot. It covered just the edge of the park, and he finally saw the second and third gunmen come into view.

And he also saw Nicole.

She was coming from the other side. No car. She was on foot, but it was possible she'd parked a vehicle somewhere nearby. If so, the deputies would find it, and it could be processed for evidence.

Drury continued to watch as Nicole moved

closer to the spot where she'd called out to them. She was staying low, looking all around her. Definitely the way a frightened person would be acting, but that didn't mean this wasn't all just that—an act. Especially since Nicole was clearly staying out of Lucas's and Kade's line of sight. In fact, so were the gunmen. That meant they must have scoped out the place beforehand and knew just where to position themselves.

Nicole ducked behind those shrubs, and Drury tried to calculate the angle of the gunmen. The guy in the tree would have definitely seen her. Probably the other two as well, but they hadn't tried to take or shoot her. So, why wait?

Drury didn't like the answer that came to mind, and it twisted at his gut.

Because maybe the thugs were waiting for Nicole to lure Caitlyn out of hiding.

It was less than a minute before Drury saw when he'd opened the door. There was no audio on the feed, but he could tell from their reactions as Nicole had called out for them not to shoot. Seconds later, the shots had started, and Grayson, Caitlyn and he had been pinned down.

"What is that?" Caitlyn asked, pointing to the camera feed from the right side of the building.

Drury had been so focused on the gunmen and all the shooting that he'd missed it. But he didn't miss it now. It was just a glimpse of a man, and like the others he was dressed in black and wearing a ski mask. Skulking along just at the edge of the parking lot, he aimed something at the camera. The screen flickered, and not just a little motion, either. The man had jammed it so that the images were clouded with static.

"Why would he have done that?" Caitlyn looked up at Drury for answers.

Answers he didn't have. It didn't make sense to jam the camera on that side, not when the other camera was capturing the shooters and Nicole.

Drury leaned in, hoping to pick through all the static to catch sight of the man. And he did. Fragments that he had to piece together. The man was on all fours, crawling toward the back door of the sheriff's office.

Maybe.

If he'd come at them from that angle, they wouldn't have been able to see him. Neither would Kade or Lucas. So, why hadn't he attacked?

"He took something from his pocket," Caitlyn said at the exact moment that Drury caught the motion.

It was small enough to fit in the palm of his hand, and it wasn't a gun. Nor was it the same device he'd pointed at the camera. A few seconds later, Drury saw what the man did with it.

He placed it beneath the rear of the car and then scurried back to the side of the building before he stood and took off running. Not toward them. But away from the sheriff's office.

"You think it's a tracking device?" Caitlyn asked.

No. Something worse. "I think it's a bomb."

Caitlyn didn't have much color in her face, and that didn't help. "Stay here," he warned her.

Drury hurried out of the office and made a beeline for the back exit just off the break room. The door was slightly ajar, and Lucas and Kade were back there with a CSI team. So was the car. It was still parked right where his brother had left it when they'd come inside after the attack.

"I think there's an explosive device on the car," Drury warned them.

Lucas cursed, and he quickly relayed the warning to the CSIs. All of them scrambled inside the break room and then toward the front of the building just as soon as Lucas kicked the door shut.

"I'll call the bomb squad," Lucas volunteered.

While his brother did that, they all got as far away from the car as they could while remaining inside.

Hell. Drury thought this was over, and it was possible that it was just beginning. If it was indeed a bomb, it could blast through the building.

Gage went out front, no doubt to make sure the area stayed clear. Both the building and the parking lot were roped off with crime scene tape, but they had to make sure gawkers weren't too close just in case the device detonated.

Caitlyn and Drury went back into Grayson's office and shut the door. Not only in case of a possible explosion but also because Helen was peering out of the interview room. And she was cursing them because she was in danger.

"The gunmen probably intended to set it off once we were in the car," Caitlyn said.

He couldn't disagree with that. But there was an even worse possibility. It could have been timed to go off once they arrived back at the ranch. If so, the baby could have been hurt. Hell, a lot of people could have been hurt.

If that was the intention, then that led him right back to Jeremy.

Jeremy was the only one of their suspects with a strong motive to get rid of his brother's heir. Of course, Melanie might not be too thrilled about it, either. Still, it didn't rule out Helen simply because the bomb might have been rigged to have another go at murdering Caitlyn.

And that meant they were back to square one.

Well, they were unless the wounded gunman somehow managed to stay alive. Then there was Ronnie. Once the bomb threat was taken care of, Grayson would no doubt figure out if Ronnie was blowing smoke or if he truly had something to make a deal.

All of those thoughts were racing through Drury's mind, but he hadn't forgotten about Caitlyn. Now that the adrenaline was wearing off, it wouldn't be long before she crashed. There was an apartment on the second floor. More of a flop room, really, but if they ended up being stuck here for a while, he might be able to coax her into getting some rest.

Alone.

With all the energy still zinging between them, it definitely wouldn't be a good idea for him to get close to her right now. Caitlyn had a different notion about that, though. She stood, slipping right into his arms, and she dropped her head against his shoulder.

"Don't you dare apologize," Drury warned her. "Because none of this is your fault."

"This is my fault," she argued, and Caitlyn glanced at the now-close contact between them.

Yes, it was, but that still didn't cause Drury to back away from her. No way could he do that because this was soothing his nerves as much as he hoped it was soothing hers. It wouldn't last, of course. Because he knew the comfort would turn into so much more.

Even now he wanted her.

Hell, he always wanted her, and he couldn't seem to get it through his thick skull that being with her could complicate his life in the worst possible way. Drury wasn't sure how long they stood there, but the sound of his phone buzzing had him finally breaking the contact. He expected to see his brother's name on the screen, but his chest tightened when he saw that the caller had blocked his identity and number.

Caitlyn saw it, too, and she sucked in her breath. "Put it on speaker," she insisted.

Drury did, but he would have preferred to buffer any bad news, and he figured this would fall into the bad news category. He hit the answer button but waited for the caller to speak first.

"Agent Ryland?" a man said. Drury couldn't be sure, but it sounded like the same person who'd fired shots at them. The one who'd taken Nicole at gunpoint.

"Where's Nicole?" Drury snapped.

"Alive for now. If you want her to stay that way, then I'll be needing some cash. Lots of it. I know she's not Ryland kin. Hell, she's probably not even someone you're sure you can trust, but hear this, I will kill her if you don't pay up."

The caller was right about Drury not being certain that he could trust Nicole, but there was something in this guy's voice. Something to let Drury know that he would indeed kill the surrogate.

"How much?" Drury asked.

"I'm lettin' you off cheap. A quarter of a million. Chump change for folks like you and Caitlyn."

"Caitlyn's already drained her accounts paying the ransom for the baby. And why should I pay? The surrogate is nothing to me."

It was a bluff, of course. She was something to him. Not just because she was a human being who probably needed protection, but also because Nicole could perhaps give them answers that would put this thug and his boss in jail for the rest of their miserable lives.

"You'll pay," the man answered, "because you're one of the good guys. A real cowboy cop with a code of honor and junk like that. I, however, have no such code. Start scraping together the money, and I'll call you back with instructions on how this drop will happen."

"I want to talk to Nicole. I want to make sure she's all right," Drury countered.

"She's all right," the guy snapped.

"Then prove it," Drury snapped right back.

The guy cursed, and a few seconds dragged by before Drury heard something he didn't want to hear.

Nicole.

Screaming.

Chapter Fifteen

No matter how much she tried to shut it out, Caitlyn couldn't stop Nicole's scream from replaying in her head. Couldn't stop the fears she had about the woman's safety, either.

She could be dead.

They had no way of knowing because right after that scream, the kidnapper had ended the call. It was possible that he'd killed her on the spot, but Caitlyn was praying that he'd only frightened Nicole into making that bloodcurdling sound. After all, if Nicole was dead, he wouldn't get the quarter-of-a-million-dollar ransom. Maybe that alone would be enough for him to keep her alive.

She sank down onto the bed of the small second-floor apartment where Drury had told her to wait. It was definitely bare bones, a place for the cops to rest when pulling long shifts.

Like now.

All the Silver Creek lawmen, including Drury, were scrambling to remedy this nightmare, and she figured they wouldn't be doing much sleeping until they made an arrest.

Whenever that would be.

She finished the sandwich that Drury had brought her earlier. Not because she was hungry. She wasn't, and her stomach was still in knots. But she didn't want to give him anything else to worry about since he'd insisted that she eat something.

The bone-weary fatigue was catching up with her fast, so Caitlyn went to the small bathroom and splashed some water on her face. It didn't help, but nothing would at this point. Well, nothing other than the person behind this being caught so everyone could try to get on with their normal lives.

For her, though, it'd be a new normal.

Since Grant's death, she'd been working again as a CPA and had a full list of clients. That would have to change since she wanted to spend as much time as she could with Caroline. She was looking forward to that.

Not looking forward, though, to dealing with the fallout from Drury.

And there would be fallout. Caitlyn wasn't sure how she was going to get over this broken heart. Nor was she sure she could stop herself from falling in love with him. Talk about stupid. But it was as if she had no choice in any of this.

She wiped away a fresh set of tears when she heard someone coming up the steps that led to the apartment. As Drury had instructed, she'd locked the door, and she didn't jump to open it. Not until she heard Drury's voice, that is.

"It's me," he said, and he relocked it as soon as he let him in. It was just a precaution, he'd assured her, but Caitlyn knew he had to be concerned about another attack. She certainly was.

"Bad news?" she asked.

He shook his head. "Nothing from the kidnapper anyway. But the bomb's been disarmed. No one was hurt."

Good. There'd been enough people hurt. "Was the bomb on a timer?"

"No, it was rigged with a remote control, and there weren't enough explosives to blow up the car, only to disable it."

It took Caitlyn a moment to process that. "You think they wanted us stranded on the road?"

"That's my guess. That's why Grayson's having all the roads and ditches checked between here and the ranch. It might take a while, though." He paused. "That means we might have to stay here all night."

Part of her had already figured that out, but it didn't hurt any less.

He brushed a kiss on her cheek, got the laptop from the desk and brought it to her. He sat down on the bed next to her. "I thought maybe you'd like to see the baby. Tillie is setting up the video feed. It should be ready any second now."

Drury had managed to make her feel as if she were melting when he kissed her, but this was a melting feeling of a different kind. Caitlyn was so touched that she kissed him even before she knew she was going to do it.

It was a good thing that the movement on the screen stopped the kiss before it had a chance to catch fire. A good thing, too, because Caitlyn soon saw her precious baby on the screen.

"She had a bottle about ten minutes ago," Tillie said. She wasn't on camera. Only Caroline, who was sleeping in the bassinet that one of the Ryland brothers had brought over, was.

"Has she cried much?" Caitlyn asked.

"Hardly at all. And she's got such a sweet disposition. So calm. Unlike Mason's boys. Those two can run you ragged pretty fast."

"They can," Drury agreed. "Max and Matt. When they team up with Gage's boy, Dustin, all the nannies at Silver Creek Ranch have to join forces just to keep them out of trouble."

Caitlyn smiled through the happy tears. The conversation was something that families had all the time, and since she'd lost both her parents when she was young, she'd missed this. Missed having the support system that Gage and Mason clearly had.

Drury, too.

"Thank you for watching her," Caitlyn said. "I know you have plenty of other things you could be doing."

Tillie went to the side of the bassinet so that Caitlyn could see her. "She's no trouble at all. Besides, we're in between newborns at the ranch right now. A rarity, I can tell you, and newborns are my favorite."

Caitlyn was thankful for that, but she still wished she was the one there taking care of her.

"Soon," Drury whispered, slipping his hand over hers.

Caitlyn wasn't sure if Tillie could see the gesture, but she smiled. "Lynette's coming over to get some cuddle time and to spend the night," she went on. "That's Gage's wife."

"Yes, I remember her." She owned the town's newspaper. "Uh, is it safe for her to be outside, though?"

"The ranch is under heavy guard right now. Mason even hired some private security to patrol the fence. Don't worry, Lynette will be careful. We'll all be careful," Tillie added.

Caroline squirmed and made a face, and Caitlyn watched as the nanny scooped her up in her arms. "I think it's time for a diaper change. Tell you what, if you're still stuck in town come morning, we'll have another computer chat over her morning bottle."

Caitlyn thanked the woman again, blew her daughter a kiss and watched until the screen went blank. Almost immediately, she felt the loss. Mercy, these were the moments she should be spending with her daughter.

"I'm sorry," Drury said, putting the laptop aside. "I thought it might make you feel better."

"It did." She wiped away the tears. "Seeing her helped."

"You're sure about that?" He used his thumb to brush away a tear on her cheek that she'd missed.

She tried to force a smile. Was sure she failed. Was also sure she shouldn't start this conversation, but Caitlyn did anyway.

"Do you think of Lily when you see the baby?" she asked.

Drury looked away, dodging her gaze for a couple of seconds, and she was certain the answer was yes. It cut her to the core to think what this was doing to him.

"No," he said.

Oh. And she added another "oh" when their eyes met again. That wasn't the look of a man dealing with the old memories.

"Sometimes, it'd be easier if I did think of her,"

he added. "Because then I wouldn't feel this guilt that I'm forgetting her."

"You'll never forget her," Caitlyn assured him.

He made a sound that could have meant anything and then groaned softly. Caitlyn was sure he would find an excuse to leave so he could deal with these feelings that were causing chaos inside him.

But he didn't leave.

Drury stared at her. "If you're going to stop this, stop it now."

She knew exactly what he meant by *this*. Sex. They'd been skirting around it for days. Heck, for years. Now the fire was burning even hotter than ever, and the walls they'd built between them were crumbling fast.

Caitlyn shook her head, almost afraid to trust her voice. "I'm not stopping it."

She couldn't tell if that pleased Drury or not. But he must have accepted it because he slid his hand around the back of her neck and pulled her to him.

DRURY DIDN'T ALLOW himself to consider that this was a mistake. Everything he did with Caitlyn seemed to fall into that category, and he was tired of fighting this attraction. This need. Tired of fighting with himself, too.

Apparently, Caitlyn felt the same way because

she moved right into the kiss. Before his mouth touched her, all Drury had felt was the spent adrenaline and the bitter taste of what would be regret.

The kiss erased them both.

Caitlyn somehow managed to rid him of the remaining doubts along with heating up every inch of his body. He didn't believe in magic or miracles, but she could weave some kind of spell around him. She'd always been able to do that.

She slipped her arms around him and pulled him closer. Not that she had to urge him to do that. Drury was already heading in that direction anyway. And he continued moving, continued kissing her until there was no way for them to get any closer. Well, not with their clothes on anyway.

"Don't stop," Caitlyn warned him.

A good man would have. Or at least a sensible one would have. But Drury wasn't in a good, sensible place right now. He was in an apartment, the door was locked, and even though they could get interrupted, he'd go with this and try to put out this raging fire they'd started.

He took the kisses to her neck and got the exact reaction he wanted. Caitlyn made that silky sound of pleasure. He knew there were other places where he could get the same reaction from her, and Drury wished he had time to rediscover them all. But there wouldn't be much time for foreplay tonight.

Maybe next time.

That thought didn't give him much comfort. Because there might not be a next time, and even if there was, next times came with even more complications. Sex couldn't be just sex with Caitlyn.

He shoved up her top and went even lower with his next round of kisses. To the tops of her breasts. She repeated the sound, kicking the heat into overdrive. Apparently kicking up her own need, too, because Caitlyn kissed him right back. On his neck. His chest.

That sure didn't slow things down.

Along with the raging need, Drury could feel everything speeding up. Not just for him but for Caitlyn. Her hands were trembling, hurried, when she took off his shoulder holster. Drury helped. Helped with his shirt, too, though he didn't manage to get it off, only unbuttoned.

Because Caitlyn went after his zipper.

"Please tell me you have a condom," she said.

"Wallet," he managed to answer.

She rummaged around for that while Drury pulled off her top. Then her bra. No way could he pass up her breasts, so he dropped some kisses there despite the fact that Caitlyn seemed hellbent on finishing this off now.

Drury hated that this felt like some kind of race. Hated that it would only cool the fire temporarily. But that hate vanished in a split second when Caitlyn peeled off her jeans and underwear. Then his. Seeing her naked was a way to rid him of any doubts he had about this. A way to rid him of every thought that had been in his head.

He took her.

Drury pulled her back onto the bed with him with only one thought in mind. Finish this. So that's what he did.

Their bodies automatically adjusted, and he eased into her. He had to take a moment, to rein in his body. To settle himself. But he also took a moment just to enjoy the feel of her. Always pleasure.

Always something more.

The *more* fueled him. Not that he needed anything else now. He had plenty of motivation.

The years melted away, and they fell right into the old rhythm. The one that would end all of this much too soon. Drury tried to hold on to each sensation, each sound that she made. The taste of her.

Each moment.

He kissed her when she shattered and gathered her close. That was all he needed.

Just Caitlyn.

Drury held on to her and shattered right along with her.

Chapter Sixteen

Caitlyn had been certain that she wouldn't be able to sleep. Not with the insanity that had been going on. And especially not with Drury in the bed with her. But when she woke up and looked at the clock, she realized it was already past midnight.

Four hours of sleep might not sound like much, but it was the most rest she'd gotten since this whole ordeal had started.

She could thank Drury in part for that.

The sex had calmed her nerves along with giving her the pleasure that she knew Drury was plenty capable of giving. The trouble was she wanted more of that pleasure. She wanted more of him.

He was still next to her in the small bed. A surprise. Though he was no longer naked. Sometime after she'd fallen asleep, he'd gotten dressed. Probably because the building was full of Ryland lawmen. That reminder was her cue to get dressed as well.

Caitlyn tried not to make a sound, but the moment she moved, Drury's eyes flew open.

"They'll knock first before they try the door," he said, sounding very wide-awake. "And the door is locked."

Yes, she knew that. "If they knock, I don't want them to hear me scrambling around in here for my clothes."

Of course, she also didn't want to climb out of the bed naked and dress with Drury watching her.

"They'll know we've had sex," Drury added. "I don't know how they'll know, but they will."

Caitlyn didn't doubt that. There seemed to be a deep connection between Drury and his cousins and brothers. She'd witnessed many instances where unspoken things had passed between them with just simple glances.

She nodded, and despite the being-naked part, she got up anyway, gathered up her clothes and took them to the bathroom so she could freshen up and dress. Caitlyn figured she was in there only five minutes or less, but when she came back out, Drury was not only up, he was making a fresh pot of coffee and was looking at something on the laptop.

"Did something happen?" she asked.

The corner of his mouth lifted for just a moment, and Drury glanced at the bed.

"Did something happen other than the obvious?" Caitlyn amended. "I know what went on there."

Now Drury's gaze came to hers. "Do you? Because I'm still trying to figure it out."

This seemed like much too deep of a post-sex question, so she went to the coffeepot and poured them both a cup.

"I, uh, don't want you to think this means something," she said. "I mean, it does mean something. To me." Mercy, she was babbling. "I just don't expect you to have to feel the same way. In fact, you don't have to feel any way at all."

Yes, definite babbling.

Drury's expression didn't change even though he was staring at her, and just when Caitlyn thought he was going to sit there and let her keep talking, he stood, brushed a kiss on her mouth.

A kiss so hot that it could have melted chrome.

"It meant something to me, too," he said in that hot and cowboy way that only Drury could have managed.

But she didn't get a chance to ask him what he meant by that because there was a knock at the door. When Drury opened the door, she saw Mason standing there. Since he was only a reserve deputy these days, it meant Grayson had to be plenty busy to call him out, and Mason didn't look very happy about it. Of course, Mason wasn't the looking-happy-about-anything sort.

"The roads are clear," Mason greeted. "No guarantees, of course, but there are no signs of the kidnappers or idiot clowns who want to shoot at you. That means you can head back to the ranch, unless you're busy…" He glanced at the unmade bed. Then he turned those glances on Drury and her.

Yes, Mason knew all right.

"You ready to leave?" Drury asked her.

"More than ready. I want to see my daughter."

"I figured you would." Mason started down the stairs, and they followed him. "Gage had to leave. Lynette's having labor pains. Somebody's always having labor pains at the ranch," he added, though he didn't seem upset that it had caused him to be called into work.

However, Drury's forehead bunched up. "Isn't it a little early for Lynette to be having the babies?"

Mason shrugged. "The doc said twins can come early."

Drury didn't exactly seem comforted by that. Maybe because it brought back memories of Lily. The sex upstairs wouldn't have helped with that, either, and Caitlyn suspected it wouldn't be long before he would feel guilty. Almost as if he'd cheated on his wife.

"Is Lynette having boys, girls or one of each?" Caitlyn asked.

"Boys," Mason answered. "No shortage of those at Silver Creek Ranch." He looked back at her. "Having your little girl there is a nice change. Not just for Drury but for all of us."

Caitlyn couldn't be sure, but she thought maybe that was some kind of hint that she was welcome there. Or maybe even more than that. Was he matchmaking?

No, she had to be wrong about that.

When they made it to the squad room, Caitlyn immediately spotted the car parked right outside the front door. "It's not a cop car," Drury explained. "It's one of Mason's."

"Is it bullet resistant?" she quickly asked.

He nodded. "Mason had it modified, and I'm hoping that since it doesn't look like a cop car, we won't be followed."

She hoped that, as well.

Drury didn't have to tell her to move fast. Every second out in the open was a second they could be gunned down, so she hurried into the backseat of the car with Drury following.

However, Mason didn't join them. Deputy Kara Duggan was behind the wheel, and Dade was rid-ing shotgun. The moment Drury and she were inside, Kara took off.

"We need to take the long way," Dade informed them. "Just to make sure no one is following us."

As much as Caitlyn hated spending any more time away from Caroline, this precaution was one she welcomed. She definitely didn't want to lead those armed thugs back to the ranch.

Dade glanced back at Drury. "The safe house is finally ready. Just as you requested, first thing in the morning the Rangers will be taking over the protection detail for Caitlyn and the baby."

That brought on an uncomfortable silence. Drury had made those arrangements before, well, *before*, and maybe he wasn't regretting them now. Or not. He could want some space so he could sort through everything that'd happened.

"Of course, I can cancel the Rangers if you'd rather keep them in your protective custody," Dade added.

Even in the darkness, Caitlyn had no trouble seeing Dade's half smile. So maybe he wasn't totally opposed to Drury being with her. But that didn't mean the Rylands would welcome her with open arms. Heck, it didn't mean Drury would, either.

"Was there some kind of family meeting about Caitlyn?" Drury came out and asked.

"Some things were mentioned," Dade admitted. "The wives got involved."

And with that cryptic comment, Dade turned in the seat to look at her. "They seem to think we've all been too rough on you. Of course, there's the part about you drop-kicking Drury's heart, but the *suggestion* I got was that everyone deserves a fresh start."

Drury opened his mouth but didn't get a chance to answer because his phone buzzed. Caitlyn was close enough to see the blocked caller on the screen, and her stomach dropped. No. Not another call from the kidnappers.

"I'll record it," Dade offered, and he pressed the button on his phone to do that just as Drury took the call and put it on speaker.

"Drury?" she heard the caller say.

It was Nicole.

"Are you okay?" Drury immediately asked.

"For now. I escaped, and I stole the kidnapper's phone so I could call you. You have to help me, Drury. You have to help me now."

Drury groaned softly. Not because he wasn't relieved that Nicole was alive, but because he didn't want to do this with her in the car.

"Where are you?" Drury demanded.

"Nearby. Pull over right now."

Caitlyn glanced around. They were at the end

of Main Street where there was only a handful of businesses. All closed for the night.

"Should I stop?" Kara asked.

She could practically see the debate going on inside Drury and Dade, and like her, they were trying to pick through the dimly lit street.

And Caitlyn finally saw her.

Sweet heaven.

Nicole staggered out from between two buildings, and Caitlyn got just a glimpse of the woman's bloody, battered face before Nicole collapsed onto the ground.

"DON'T YOU DARE get out of the car," Drury warned Caitlyn when she reached for the door handle.

She was probably running on pure instinct to help an injured woman, but it was possible that Nicole wasn't even hurt.

Or if she really was hurt, she could be bait.

Either scenario wasn't good because it meant someone was going to try to ambush them.

"I'll call Grayson so we can get some help out here," Dade said, taking out his phone.

"Please help me," Nicole begged. At least she sounded as if she were begging, but Drury wasn't about to trust any of this.

"Where are the men who kidnapped you?" he asked.

Nicole didn't answer right away. All he could

hear was her ragged breath, and she lifted her head, only for it to drop back down again. It twisted at him to think she could be truly injured and that he was just sitting there. But he didn't have a lot of options here.

"I ran from them," Nicole finally said. "They were going to kill me after they got the ransom. I heard them say it. They were going to kill both Caitlyn and me."

"Why Caitlyn?" Drury pressed.

Nicole lifted her head again. Shook it. "I don't know, but I think they want the baby. Please don't let them have the baby."

"I won't," Caitlyn quickly assured her. That's when Drury realized she was trembling. Of course, she had a good reason to do that since she'd just heard that someone was out to kill her. If they were to believe Nicole, that is.

"Grayson's on the way," Dade relayed when he ended the call.

Both Kara and he already had their guns drawn. Drury, too. And they had them aimed at Nicole. Like the others, Drury also continued to look around to make sure no one was trying to sneak up on them. As soon as backup arrived, he wanted to get Caitlyn out of there.

"Watch the tops of the buildings," Drury told Dade, and Drury turned his attention back to Nicole. "How bad are you hurt?"

"Bad. I think one of the thugs broke some of my ribs. I'm in a lot of pain." She moaned again.

"Why did they only hit you?" Drury pressed. "If they wanted to kill you, they could have just shot you." He heard his own words and mentally cringed. Definitely not kid-glove treatment, but he had to treat her like a suspect until he was positive that she wasn't.

"They were holding me just a few blocks from here, and I ran when they stepped away to make a phone call. They caught up with me, and the big guy tackled me. Then he punched me. He would have killed me, but I kicked him between his legs and ran. I came here because I need you to help me."

Yeah, she'd made that clear. "Help is on the way."

She lifted her head, looked at him. He expected her to demand that he allow her in the car. Something that would give her or those thugs easy access to Caitlyn. But she didn't.

"Thank you," Nicole said, and she lay her head back down.

Dade's phone rang, the shrill sound shooting through the car and causing Caitlyn to gasp. Obviously she was as much on edge as he was. Dade didn't put the call on speaker, maybe because he didn't want the call to drown out any sounds they might need to hear.

Like footsteps.

But only a few seconds into the conversation, Dade cursed, and Drury knew they had more trouble on their hands.

"Grayson said someone set fires on Main Street," Dade told them, and now he pressed the speaker button so they could hear the rest from Grayson himself.

"It's a wall of flames right now in both directions," Grayson went on. "I have no way of reaching you, except on foot."

Hell. That was not what Drury wanted to hear. It meant backup couldn't get to them, and he figured that wasn't an accident. No. This was all part of someone's sick plan to get to Caitlyn.

"My advice is to get out of there," Grayson went on. "Fast. I'll get to Nicole as soon as I can."

Which might not be very soon. Or in time. Because if she was truly innocent in all of this, she would be easy prey for the kidnappers to finish off.

"Someone's on the roof," Kara said, and she pointed to the building across the street. "And he's got a gun."

"Get down on the seat," Drury told Caitlyn.

Because of his position, he had to lean down to see the shooter on the roof. He was in the shadows, but Drury had no trouble figuring out where the guy was aiming. Not at the car.

But rather at Nicole.

Oh, man. This thug was going to gun her down. Nicole must have seen him, too, because she managed a strangled scream and got to her feet. She staggered toward the car.

There was no time for Drury to debate what he had to do. No time for anything because the first shot rang out and blasted into the sidewalk, just a few inches from Nicole.

Nicole kept coming toward the car. Kept screaming for help, too. And knowing it was a decision that he could instantly regret, Drury opened the door. He took hold of Nicole's arm and pulled her inside.

"Go now!" Drury shouted to Kara.

The deputy sped off as the bullets slammed into the car.

Chapter Seventeen

Caitlyn's heart went into overdrive, but she figured she wasn't the only one in the cruiser with that reaction. The bullets were coming right at them, and it was possible they'd just let one of their attackers into the car.

"Go faster," Nicole insisted. "They'll kill us all."

Nicole certainly sounded terrified. Looked it, too. Caitlyn peered around Drury so she could see the woman. And she saw her all right. Nicole's face was a bloody mess, and judging from her ragged breath and wincing, she was in a lot of pain.

Kara did hit the accelerator, and the tires of the cruiser squealed as the deputy turned off Main Street. Caitlyn couldn't tell where she was going, but she prayed they could outrun whoever was attacking them.

"I have to frisk you," Drury told Nicole. "Put

your hands on your head and don't make any sudden moves."

The woman didn't object. Nicole just nodded and did as he'd instructed. Drury kept himself positioned between Nicole and her while he checked the surrogate for weapons.

"She's not armed," Drury told them after he'd finished.

Caitlyn released the breath she'd been holding, but she didn't feel much relief. Since Nicole wasn't armed and she was injured, it meant she'd likely been telling the truth. It also meant she needed medical attention.

"Call the hospital," Drury told Dade. "If the shooter isn't tailing us, we'll take Nicole to the ER."

It was necessary, but Caitlyn knew it wouldn't necessarily be safe. For any of them. After all, an armed thug had gotten into the hospital to take Ronnie, and while that particular kidnapping had been fake, it was a reminder of just how easy it would be for a gunman to get inside.

If one wasn't already there.

In fact, those thugs could have injured Nicole as a way to lure them all into a trap.

Caitlyn looked at Drury to tell him that, but judging from his expression, he already knew.

"We've got a tail," Kara warned them.

Even though Drury pushed both Nicole and

her lower on the seat, Caitlyn managed to get a glimpse of the SUV that was coming up fast behind them. It was too much to hope that it was someone from the sheriff's office who'd made it through that fiery roadblock.

"Something's wrong with my phone," Dade said. "I'm not getting a signal."

Caitlyn hoped it was just a matter of them being in a dead zone. There were some places in Texas where you couldn't use a cell phone, but they were just outside town where that shouldn't have been a problem.

While still volleying his attention between Nicole and that SUV, Drury took out his phone and handed it to Caitlyn. "See if I've got any bars."

Her stomach sank when she saw no signal on the screen. She shook her head. "Nothing."

Several seconds later, Kara verified the same.

No. Now they had no way to get in touch with Grayson and the others to tell them where they were heading. Once they knew where they were heading, that is. Right now, their only goal was to escape before this attack escalated.

"Maybe the SUV's got some kind of jamming device aimed at us," Dade suggested.

That didn't help with her nerves. "Is that even possible?"

A muscle flickered in Drury's jaw. "Yeah. I've seen devices that can shut down services for up to a mile. Any chance you can put some distance between us and the SUV?" he asked Kara.

"I'll try." She slowed, only so she could make another turn, and gunned the engine again.

The problem with getting away from the SUV, though, was that they were heading farther and farther away from town. And they couldn't go to the ranch. Not with possible gunmen in pursuit. At least the men weren't shooting at them.

Not now anyway.

But Caitlyn figured that probably wouldn't last. Added to that, the men probably had their own backup all over the area. There weren't that many roads in this part of the county, and they could have someone stashed on each one of them. Of course, that meant those *someones* had stayed hidden when Mason and the others had been checking the roads.

Drury glanced at Nicole again. "Did the men who kidnapped you have you in that SUV?"

She dragged in a long breath and looked back at the vehicle. "I think so, yes. But I didn't see any kind of equipment in it that could jam phones. They had a lot of guns, though."

"Think hard," Drury pressed. "Is there anything about them that will help us out of this situation?"

She started shaking her head again but then

stopped. "One of them is injured. He fell when they were chasing me, and he hurt his shoulder."

It wasn't much, but maybe it would be enough if it came down to a face-to-face showdown. Of course, maybe there were more than two men in that SUV.

Drury tipped his head to his phone that Caitlyn was still holding. "Keep checking the phone to see if we get a signal, but stay down."

The words had no sooner left his mouth when Caitlyn heard a sound she definitely didn't want to hear.

A gunshot.

The bullet crashed into the back windshield. The glass held, but it cracked and webbed.

Another shot.

Then another.

Both tore into the glass even more, and Caitlyn knew it wouldn't be long before the bullets made it through.

"Hold on," Kara said a split second before she slammed on the brakes so she could take another turn.

Caitlyn was wearing her seat belt, but she still slammed against Drury, and Nicole hit the window and door, causing her to make a sharp sound of pain. She obviously needed to get to the hospital, but that couldn't happen until they lost the goons behind them.

"Still no phone signal," Caitlyn relayed to them after she checked the screen again. She'd hoped that the turn Kara had made would have been enough to lose the jammer. But no such luck.

She got proof of that when the next shot bashed into the window.

"The shooter's leaning out the passenger's-side door," Dade said, looking in the mirror. "Let me see if I can do something to stop him."

"Be careful," Drury warned him, and he looked at Nicole. "I need you to move next to Caitlyn so I can try to take out the driver from this window. So help me, you'd better be an innocent victim in all of this."

"I am. I swear, I am."

Drury apparently didn't take that as gospel because he took out his backup weapon and handed it to Caitlyn. "Watch her," he said.

Caitlyn would, along with keeping an eye on the phone screen, but now she had a new distraction. Drury was putting himself right in the path of those bullets, and there wouldn't be any glass to protect him.

Drury maneuvered himself around Nicole, putting the woman in the middle of the seat, and he lowered the window. Leaned out. And fired.

From the other side of the car Dade did the same.

Both got off several shots, and that seemed to

do the trick of stopping the gunman from continuing to fire. Now if they could just get away from them and regroup.

"Hell." Drury added more profanity to that. So did Dade. Both of them quit shooting and dropped back in their seats.

And Caitlyn soon figured out why.

The SUV rammed into the rear of their car.

DRURY HAD SEEN the impact coming. Had tried to stop it from hurting Caitlyn and Nicole, but he failed. The jolt slung them around like rag dolls, and even though Caitlyn was wearing a seat belt, her body still snapped forward.

Nicole yelped in pain. Heaven knew what this was doing to her if she truly did have broken ribs. An impact like that could puncture a lung.

And worse, it didn't stop.

The driver of the SUV plowed into them again. Then again.

Drury glanced back, hoping like the devil that the collisions were tearing up the front of the SUV, but it must have been reinforced because he couldn't see any damage at all.

Unlike their car.

The back end was bashed in, and the windows were holding by a thread. The SUV and the bullets were tearing the vehicle apart. Which was no doubt the plan. After that, these thugs could pick them off one by one.

"Still no signal on the phone," Caitlyn said, though he wasn't sure how she managed to speak. Especially not when the SUV rammed into them again.

This was obviously a well-thought-out plan, and they'd been waiting for Caitlyn and him to leave the sheriff's office. In hindsight, that was a mistake. Of course, there could be an attack going on there, too. With Ronnie in the building, his comrades might try to break him out of jail.

"I'm turning on Millington Road," Kara told them. She was fighting with the steering wheel, doing her best to keep them out of the ditch— where the SUV driver was apparently trying to force them to go.

Just when Drury thought it couldn't get any worse, it did.

After the SUV rammed them again, the shots returned. The shooter was barely leaning out of the window, and he started sending a spray of bullets into the back windshield.

"Oh, God," Kara said.

Drury's gaze whipped in her direction to see what'd caused that reaction, and he soon saw it. A fire just ahead. And it stretched across the entire width of the farm road. Drury hadn't seen the fires that Grayson had described near the sheriff's office, but he suspected this one was identical to those.

Set by the same people.

People who clearly wanted them dead.

Kara slammed on the brakes, and even though they were still a good forty feet from the fire, the wind was whipping the smoke in their direction. They couldn't see far enough to know how deep those flames extended, which meant they were now officially sitting ducks.

The SUV braked, too, but it wasn't nearly enough. It slammed into them again. The hardest impact of all, and this time it didn't just send them flying around. The car jolted.

Because it wound up in a ditch.

The car immediately tilted, the tires on the passenger's side sinking deep into the ditch. Drury figured these thugs weren't just going to drive off and leave them there. They also had help nearby because after all, someone had set that fire.

"Keep watch around us," Drury warned them.

They did. Caitlyn, too. She still had his phone in her left hand and continued to check it for a signal. Which they likely weren't going to get out here. No jamming equipment needed since this spot was far away from any houses and not close enough to the tower for them to have service.

Part of this sick plan, no doubt.

But the question was—how would they get out of this?

They were probably outnumbered, but there were two cops and an FBI agent in the car. Plus, Caitlyn was armed, though he hoped it didn't come down to her having to shoot.

However, the men in the SUV didn't get out.

Maybe Nicole had been right about one of them being hurt. Or they could be just waiting for the rest of their thug crew to arrive.

"We can't just sit here," Drury said, talking more to himself than the others.

He looked around to try to figure out how to do this, but there weren't many options. They couldn't get out on the driver's side because that would mean they'd be on the road. With the SUV right there, they'd be gunned down the moment they stepped from the car.

That left the ditch.

Both doors were blocked on the passenger's side because of the way the car was wedged in, but there was another way out.

"We can crawl out the windows," Drury suggested. "Once we're out, we can use the ditch for cover." Actually, it was more than a suggestion. It was their only option.

Caitlyn and Dade didn't waste any time lowering the windows, but while Drury kept watch of the SUV, he scrambled across Nicole and her. No way did he want them going out there first. He snaked his way through the window but didn't go toward the front of the car that he could use for cover. Instead, he needed to provide some cover for Caitlyn and Nicole.

Dade got out as well, and he moved back to make room for Caitlyn. Once she was out, Dade hurried her to the front.

Of course, there were no guarantees that there weren't other gunmen on that side, but at least they wouldn't be coming up the road that way because of the fire. Unfortunately, there was plenty of pasture and even some woods for killers to hide.

Kara got out, helping him with Nicole. He could tell from her labored breathing that each movement only caused her pain to spike, but there was nothing he could do about that now. This was their best chance of making it out of here alive.

Drury kept volleying glances back at the SUV, and he tried to steel himself for the bullets to start flying. But the goons didn't shoot.

Why?

Maybe because they wanted at least one of them alive? But again, he had to ask himself why.

There was a cluster of huge trees only about fifteen feet away from the ditch. Close but that would mean plenty of time out in the open. Still, if they could make it there, they could perhaps then go into the woods. The creek was less than a quarter of a mile away, and they could follow it either to the ranch or back into town.

"We could just wait here and see what they decide to do," Kara said.

"Or we could make it to those trees and use them for cover," Drury countered. The darkness and smoke would help some with that. Still, it was risky. Everything was at this point.

"Hell," Dade spat out. "We've got to move now."

Drury glanced back at the SUV, and he, too, cursed. The passenger's-side window was down now, but it wasn't a gun that the thug had aimed at them. It was some kind of launcher. Drury didn't know if it held a grenade or a firebomb, and he didn't want to find out.

"Stay low and move fast," Drury ordered. "Get to those trees." He fired a shot at the SUV with the hopes of getting the guy to duck back inside the vehicle.

It worked, but he knew their luck wouldn't hold out for long.

Caitlyn crawled out of the ditch, dragging Nicole with her. Kara helped, and while they scrambled toward the trees, Dade and Drury continued to send some rounds in the SUV. The bullets weren't making their way through the windshield, but they were holding the guy with the launcher at bay.

At first anyway.

But then the barrel of the launcher came out again. Not the shooter, though. He stayed protected behind the reinforced glass.

And Drury knew Dade and he didn't have much time.

"Run!" he shouted to Dade.

They did. They took off, heading for the trees. Not a second too soon.

Because the firebomb ripped through the car.

Chapter Eighteen

The sound of the blast roared through her, but Caitlyn didn't look back. She tightened her grip on Nicole and just kept moving as fast as she could.

She prayed, though, that Dade and Drury hadn't been hurt.

They'd stayed back, to protect the rest of them, but that could have cost them their lives. Still, Caitlyn tried not to think about that, tried not to give in to the fear that had her by the throat.

With Kara on one side of Nicole and Caitlyn on the other, they made it to the trees and ducked behind them. Caitlyn got her first good look at the effects of the explosion then.

There was nothing left of the car.

It was nothing but a ball of fire.

Of course, it created even more smoke, and this was thick and black, and it took her several heart-stopping moments to look through it and spot Drury and Dade.

Alive.

Thank heaven.

They were running toward the trees, and just when Caitlyn thought they might make it, she saw something else. Something that caused her fear to spike even more. The thug who'd launched that firebomb was leaning out the window again, and this time, he had a gun.

"Watch out!" she shouted to Drury and Dade.

But it was too late. The shot slammed through the air.

The scream wouldn't make it past her throat. It was jammed there, stalling her breath, causing the panic to rise. It didn't help when the thug fired off another round of shots.

Caitlyn couldn't tell if either had been hit, but she couldn't just hide there and watch them get gunned down. She leaned out from the tree, took aim with the backup weapon Drury had given her.

And she pulled the trigger.

She wasn't sure where the shot landed, but it must have been close enough to the shooter that it got him to duck back inside. From the side of another tree, Kara fired off a shot as well, pinning down the gunman enough so that Dade and Drury could scramble in beside them.

"Stay down," Drury immediately snapped, and

he pushed her out of the line of sight of the thug in the SUV.

Not a second too soon.

Because he fired off more rounds, each of them slamming into the spot where she'd just been. It stunned her for a second. Then terrified her. Because those bullets could have hit Drury, too.

"Keep watch all around us," Drury instructed, and he glanced at Nicole. "How's she doing?"

Nicole managed to nod, though she was holding her hands over her stomach and chest. "Just stop these monsters, *please*."

Caitlyn knew that Drury and the others would try to do that. So would she. But they didn't know what they were up against.

She glanced around at their surroundings. The night. The smoke. And way too many places for backup thugs to hide and ambush them. It sickened her to think that Drury, Kara and Dade were in grave danger because of her. These men were clearly after her. Probably Nicole, too, since she might have witnessed something while captive that could be used to identify them.

Nicole moaned, drawing Caitlyn's attention back to her. She knelt down beside her and tried to see if there was anything she could do to help her. There was a gash on her forehead that was bleeding, but it wasn't enough to be life threatening. However, the woman could have internal injuries.

"Caitlyn?" someone called out. It was the man in the SUV. The one who'd been shooting at them. "You can make this easy on your boyfriend and the cops if you just give yourself up."

"That's not going to happen," Drury shouted before she could say anything. "It's not," he repeated to her.

Caitlyn knew that Drury wasn't going to want to hear this, but she had to try anyway. "You could use me to draw them out. Then we could maybe take the SUV and get Nicole to the hospital."

As expected, Drury was shaking his head before she even finished. "They'll gun you down the second you step out into the opening."

"Maybe. But they might want to take me to the person who hired them."

Drury cursed. "That isn't helping to convince me. In fact, nothing will convince me to let you go out there."

Caitlyn went closer to him. "It could save you. It could save the others. At least consider it."

Drury's next round of profanity was much worse. "You're not going out there. Do you want to make your daughter an orphan, huh?"

It felt as if he'd slapped her. No, she didn't want that, and going out there could indeed get her killed. It ate away at her to think of her baby growing up without a parent, but this was eating away at her, too.

"We'll find another way out of this," Drury insisted. He tipped his head to the phone. "Keep checking for a signal." Before she could continue the argument, he switched his attention to Kara. "You keep watch on your right. Dade, look for anything coming up from behind. Caitlyn will make sure the left side stays clear."

Judging from the way Drury barked out those orders, there wouldn't be any compromises or debates. The glare he shot her only verified that. He knelt down by the side of the tree and pinned his attention to the SUV, so Caitlyn did the same. Except she looked in the area he'd assigned to her.

Nothing.

Well, nothing that she could see anyway. There was another cluster of trees about only ten yards away, and it was plenty thick enough for someone to be hiding there.

"Caitlyn?" the thug called out again. "Maybe this will convince you that it'll be a good idea to come with us."

The barrel of a rifle came out from the SUV, and the shots started. A string of them. The bullets slammed into the tree and sent a spray of splinters all over them. Caitlyn and the others had to shelter their eyes. Worse, the wind shifted, and the smoke started drifting their way. It wouldn't kill them, but it would be hard to aim if they were coughing.

Even though the bullets were deafening, Caitlyn volleyed her attention between the phone and the area to their left. At least she did until a slash of light caught her attention. Not coming from the trees but rather the road.

Mercy, had Grayson or the deputies found them?

She held on to that hope for several seconds. Until she heard Drury curse again. Caitlyn glanced at the SUV and saw the black car pull to a stop behind it. Since the thugs weren't shooting at the vehicle, it meant this was probably more hired killers.

"What the hell are they doing?" Dade asked.

Drury shook his head, and Caitlyn tried to follow his gaze to see what had caused that reaction. Someone stepped from the car. Yes, definitely another thug. He was dressed in all dark clothes and was wearing a ski mask.

He also had the launcher aimed at them. It wasn't the same size as the other one had used. This one was much smaller.

Caitlyn's heart slammed against her ribs because she thought it might be a grenade or another firebomb, but when it hit the ground, there wasn't a blast. Instead, it began to spew out a thick cloud of smoke.

"Are they trying to get us to run?" Kara asked.

Neither Dade nor Drury answered. They continued to keep watch. Not just on the smoke but all around them.

With everything going on, it was a miracle that Caitlyn remembered to glance down at the phone, but when she did, she saw a welcome sight.

"We have a signal," she said. "It's a weak one, but I can try to text Grayson."

"Do it," Drury insisted.

Caitlyn's hands were shaking, and it took her a few seconds to steady them. However, she'd barely gotten the message started when Drury caught onto her arm and pulled her to her feet. He immediately pivoted and took aim in the direction of the SUV.

"Run!" Drury shouted.

Dade picked up Nicole and started running, too, with Kara racing right along behind him. Caitlyn glanced back but all she saw was the milky smoke.

At first anyway.

Then she saw the man. Maybe the same one who'd fired at them from the SUV, and he had the big launcher. And he fired.

The firebomb came right at them.

CHAOS.

That one word kept repeating through Drury's head.

He fired two shots at the goon with that

launcher, but couldn't stop him in time. Now, all hell was breaking loose.

"Run!" Drury repeated to the others, and he hoped like the devil they were doing that.

He ran, too, toward the other cluster of trees that was nearest to them, but he also pulled up, pivoted and fired at their attacker. Maybe, just maybe, Drury could stop him from shooting another firebomb. Or even regular shots. At this range, the gunman would be able to pick them off.

It didn't take long, mere seconds, for the smoke to get so thick that Drury couldn't see. Plus, there was the heat from the fire.

He couldn't stay put, not out in the open like this, because those gunmen could come from that wall of smoke at any second. He also didn't want to leave the others alone any longer than necessary since they'd probably already made it to the trees. That twisting feeling in his gut let him know that this could get even uglier than it already was.

"Get behind cover now and stay down," Dade called out to them.

Drury tried to do just that, and he hoped Dade had eyes on whoever was coming after them. Drury raced to those trees, dropped down and took aim. He immediately saw one of the thugs who was positioning himself to shoot what appeared to be another firebomb.

Right at them.

Drury double-tapped the trigger, sending two shots into the guy's chest. He fell, but Drury couldn't tell if he was dead or not. He hoped so because he didn't want the idiot to get another chance to use those bombs. Of course, that didn't mean there wasn't someone else ready to take the downed thug's place.

The seconds crawled by while Drury waited for someone else to come at them. There could be a half dozen or more in the SUV and car. Heck, there could be more in these woods, and that's why Drury glanced around to get his bearings and to make sure they weren't about to be ambushed.

Kara was about three yards behind him, watching their backs. Dade had taken up position two trees over, and he was looking all around them. Nicole was flat on her back and moaning in pain.

Drury hated that he couldn't do anything to help the woman, but maybe Caitlyn had managed to send that text to Grayson so that he would have their position. Grayson wouldn't be able to get an ambulance in here, not with the possibility of shots still being fired, but he and the other deputies could help them deal with the attackers.

He glanced around to ask Caitlyn about that text.

And his breath stalled in his throat.

She wasn't there. He frantically looked around

while also trying to keep watch for the attackers, but there was no sign of her.

"Where's Caitlyn?" he asked Dade and Kara.

They, too, glanced around, and Drury could tell they didn't have a clue. His first instinct was to call out to her, but that would give away their position, so he dropped back and began to search behind every tree. Hard to do that, though, with the thick underbrush covering the ground and the smoke. It was getting even thicker now.

Hell, was Caitlyn hurt?

That revved up Drury's pulse a significant notch. In all the mayhem of them running for cover, one of the thugs could have shot her. Or maybe she hadn't made it out at all.

With his stomach twisting, Drury looked back at the other set of trees. The ones that were on fire now. If she was in the middle of that, then… But he didn't even want to go there.

Caitlyn couldn't be dead.

He heard the sound to his left. A snap of a twig maybe, and the relief flooded through him.

But not for long.

It was Caitlyn all right, but she wasn't alone. Nor was she all right. There was someone behind her. One of the ski mask–wearing goons. And he had his left arm clamped around her throat in a choke hold.

He also had a gun pointed at her head.

"Surprised to see me?" the man taunted.

That immediately caused both Dade and Kara to pivot in his direction, and they took aim just as Drury already had. But none of them had a clean shot. The man had ducked down and was using Caitlyn as a human shield.

"I'm sorry," Caitlyn said. "I didn't see him in time."

Drury hated that she felt the need to apologize. Hated, too, that look in her eyes. Fear, not just for herself but for all of them.

"You probably know what you have to do next," the man continued. "You gotta all put down your guns just like Caitlyn did."

"I didn't put mine down," she snapped. "He knocked it from my hand."

"Just doing my job, and my job includes killing her right here, right now if you don't put down those guns. Same for the bimbo on the ground. My friend wants me to give her a little payback for hurting him. Of course, she won't like my version of payback."

Drury didn't recognize the guy's voice, and it definitely wasn't one of their suspects. However, it was obvious he was connected to the men who'd taken Nicole from the back of the sheriff's office.

"Who are you working for?" Drury demanded.

The man tightened his grip on Caitlyn's throat.

"What part of my order didn't you understand? I mean, it was simple enough. Guns on the ground now!"

Drury hated to surrender his weapon because he didn't have a backup. He'd given it to Caitlyn. But Kara and Dade almost certainly had some other weapon stashed away. Weapons they would no doubt need to get all of them out of this alive.

Dade was the first to drop his gun. Then Kara. Drury finally did, too, while he continued to fire glances around them. It would be a good time for other attackers to swarm in and take them all, and if that happened, their chances of survival would drop considerably.

"Now kick the guns away so you can't get to them," the man ordered.

They did, but Drury kicked his in Nicole's direction. It was a risk since there was a slim chance she could be working with these clowns. But he doubted it. And even though she was clearly in a lot of pain, maybe she'd be able to use his gun if it came down to it.

"So, what now?" Drury asked the goon when he just stood there.

"Waiting for the boss. Shouldn't be long now."

Drury doubted the boss had anything good in mind for Caitlyn. For any of them really.

The moments crawled by, and when the wind shifted, Drury saw someone walking through the smoke. Not just one person but three. Two men both dressed in black and wearing ski masks. They were armed.

But not the person in the middle.

Hell.

So, this was the *boss*.

Chapter Nineteen

Because of the way the goon had her standing, Caitlyn couldn't see the reason Drury had cursed. But she figured it couldn't be good.

Nothing about this was good, and they'd need plenty of luck to get out of it alive.

Since Dade, Kara, Drury and even the thug holding her now had their attention focused in the direction of the road, Caitlyn considered trying something. Maybe like elbowing the guy or dropping to the ground. It might cause him to shoot, but at least his gun was still aimed at her.

Mercy, she didn't want to die. But she doubted whoever was coming would spare any of them. This way, there might be a scuffle. One that Dade, Kara and Drury could maybe win.

But why hadn't the goon already killed her?

That was the question racing through her head when Caitlyn finally saw the people making their way toward them. Two more hired guns.

And Melanie.

The woman wasn't a hostage, either. Dressed as if ready to attend a business meeting, she was walking beside the men, and even though she wasn't armed, she didn't need a gun. Not with those two hired killers.

"I got her just like you said," the goon holding Caitlyn relayed to Melanie.

"Good." Melanie barely spared the others a glance. Instead, she kept her stare on Caitlyn.

Except it was a glare.

Even in the near darkness, Caitlyn had no trouble seeing it. Melanie hated her, and while she hadn't exactly kept that hatred under wraps while they were at the sheriff's office, this was pure venom that she was now aiming at Caitlyn.

Melanie's glare was still in place when she made a sweeping glance around them. "Couldn't get your lover out of this, huh?" she directed at Drury.

"The night's not over," he countered, matching her glare for glare.

Melanie smiled as if all of this were a done deal. It wasn't. Somehow they had to fight their way out of this because if Melanie and those hired killers eliminated them, they might go to the ranch next.

"Is she still alive?" Melanie asked when she looked at Nicole.

"Yeah," the goon behind Caitlyn verified. "Wasn't sure if you wanted her kept alive or not."

"No. She's worthless to me now that I can't get any money for her."

There it was—Melanie's motive all spelled out for them. Well, her partial motive anyway. She wanted Grant's money.

"Is that why my baby was born, because you wanted me to pay for her?" Caitlyn asked. She didn't bother to contain the anger in her voice and wished she could blast this idiot to smithereens.

"Of course," Melanie readily admitted. She glanced at the others again. "And I guess you know that means it's bad news for all of you. Well, bad news for everyone but Caitlyn."

Caitlyn replayed the words to make sure she'd heard her correctly. "Why would you keep me alive?" But she immediately thought of the answer. "You want me to drain all my bank accounts and give the money to you. There isn't much left."

"I want every penny of it." Caitlyn hadn't thought Melanie's venom could get any worse, but it had. Melanie fanned her hand over the thugs. "Grant's money paid for all of this."

"And you put that money in an offshore account with my name on it," Caitlyn snapped.

Melanie shrugged. "It seemed the easiest way to cover my tracks, and there's no way you could have gotten your hands on it because you didn't know the security code I set up."

And by covering her tracks, Melanie had also tried to make Caitlyn look guilty. It hadn't worked, but she hadn't needed it to work since she had the upper hand here.

"Grant's money will pay for a whole lot more since there are some loose ends that need to be tied up," Melanie added. "And what it doesn't cover, Helen will pay for. My personal living expenses, nannies and private schools for the baby."

Everything inside Caitlyn went still. "Are you talking about nannies and private schools for my daughter?"

"She's Grant's daughter, too, and I plan to raise her as my own. That way I'll have a part of Grant. If Helen cooperates with me, then she'll get to see the child. Not here, of course. I won't be able to live here."

If the thug hadn't held her back, Caitlyn would have gone after her. "You're not getting my child."

Melanie shrugged. "We'll see about that, and I'm sure Helen will pay up when she realizes I have her granddaughter."

"Is Helen in on this?" Drury asked.

Melanie made a you've-got-to-be-kidding sound. "No, this was my plan and my plan only, but since you didn't take the bait when I planted evidence against Jeremy and her, it means you sealed everyone's fate."

Drury shook his head. "What did you do?"

Melanie actually smiled. "Jeremy deserves what he gets. Do you know he killed Grant?"

"Got any proof of that?" Drury countered.

"Jeremy talks in his sleep," Melanie said under her breath. "No way could I let him get away without being punished." She motioned toward the goon holding Caitlyn. "Come on. Bring her to the car. Kill the rest," she added to the other two. "No need to do a cleanup. I'll have the kid and will be out of the country before any of these Silver Creek lawmen figure out it's me. They'll be too busy chasing Jeremy."

She'd obviously set him up somehow, but Caitlyn didn't care about that. "How do you think you're going to get my baby?"

Melanie tipped her head to the fires. "Plenty of those. In comparison to the rest of this, firebombs don't cost much at all, and I figure if we land enough of them on the Silver Creek Ranch, the Rylands will give her up to save their own."

Clearly, she didn't know the Rylands. They'd never give up the baby. But that didn't mean plenty of them wouldn't die or get hurt trying.

It felt as if someone had clamped onto her heart and was squeezing it hard. The rage bashed at her like a violent storm, building and building until Caitlyn knew where she needed to aim that rage.

At Melanie.

Melanie turned to walk away, and the goon started moving, dragging Caitlyn along with him. Leading her to where she would no doubt be tortured and eventually killed. Of course, Drury and the others would be targets long before that. They'd die within seconds if Caitlyn didn't do something now.

She latched onto all that rage she was feeling and let it and the adrenaline fuel her. Caitlyn bashed the back of her head against the goon's face, as hard as she could. So hard that she could have sworn she saw stars. She pushed aside the pain, though, and dropped to the ground. The goon didn't drop with her, nor did he let go of the gun. He was cursing her now and latched onto her hair.

That's when all hell broke loose.

Drury lunged at the thug. Dade went after the other two, and Kara scooped up Drury's gun off the ground. She probably didn't have a clean shot, but at least one of them was armed, and maybe she could stop Melanie from getting away.

"Kill them!" Melanie screamed.

Her thugs were certainly trying to do just that. Caitlyn's attacker still had hold of her hair and was using his fierce grip to sling her around to block Drury from slugging him. Drury didn't give up, though, and he finally managed to bash the guy right in the face.

It was enough to get him to stagger back and let go of her hair.

Drury pushed her away and went after the guy, plowing right into him and sending him to the ground. Caitlyn frantically looked around for the goon's gun, and her breath stalled in her throat when she saw that he still had hold of it. Worse, he was trying to aim it at Drury.

"Do your jobs and kill them." Melanie's voice was a screech, followed by some ripe profanity. She sounded insane. And probably was.

Since Melanie wasn't armed and wasn't running, Caitlyn tuned her out for a moment and tried to help Drury.

"Stay back," Drury warned her.

He probably didn't want her to be anywhere near that gun, but she wasn't just going to let him fight this alone. Caitlyn kicked at the goon's legs. And she continued to kick until the sound of the shot stopped her cold.

Oh, mercy.

Had Drury been shot?

It seemed as if time slowed to a crawl, and the sounds in her head were a series of loud echoes. She couldn't lose Drury. Especially not like this, while he'd been trying to protect her.

Caitlyn clawed at the goon, hitting any part of him that she could reach, but that's when she realized Drury hadn't been hit. The bullet had come from behind her.

Kara.

The deputy had put a bullet in one of the thug's heads. Lifeless, he dropped to the ground.

One down, but Dade and Drury were still battling the other two attackers. She couldn't tell if either was winning, but at least Kara had a gun, and the deputy hurried closer, waiting for a shot that Caitlyn was sure she would take if she got the chance. Maybe they'd actually get out of this alive.

But that's when Caitlyn saw something she didn't want to see.

Melanie was running. Getting away. And if she reached the car or SUV, she could escape. Maybe she would even try to get to the Silver Creek Ranch and try to take Caroline.

Caitlyn went after her.

It wasn't easy. She'd burned a lot of energy hitting the thug, and the smoke didn't help. It wasn't as thick as it had been, but it cut her breath. Still, that didn't stop her. Nothing would at this point. Not even Drury shouting out to her.

"Caitlyn, come back."

He was probably concerned that there were other hired killers who would come to Melanie's aid. And maybe they would, but Caitlyn couldn't let Melanie make it to the road.

Behind her, there were two shots. She hoped they'd come from Kara or that maybe Dade and Drury had managed to get hold of a weapon. Part of her wanted to go back and see, but she had to stop Melanie.

Melanie was running a lot faster than Caitlyn thought she could, and she made it all the way to the thug whom Drury had shot before Caitlyn caught up with her. Caitlyn dived at her, catching onto Melanie's waist and dragging her to the ground.

That's when Caitlyn saw the gun.

Melanie must have grabbed it from the dead guy, but she lifted her hand, taking aim at Caitlyn.

Caitlyn didn't think. She only reacted. She hit Melanie's hand just as the woman pulled the trigger.

The shot roared through the air.

Caitlyn couldn't tell where the bullet had gone, but she prayed it hadn't hit Drury or the others. Prayed, too, that she could stop Melanie from firing again. She latched onto the woman's wrist, and even though Melanie outsized her by a good thirty pounds, Caitlyn had something to fight for.

Her daughter.

If the woman escaped, there was no telling what she might do.

Behind her, there were more shots. Caitlyn had no trouble hearing them, but she couldn't look back and see if Drury was okay.

Melanie cursed her, calling her vile names while she fought like a wildcat. She kicked and dug her fingernails into Caitlyn's hand. She drew blood, but Caitlyn drew blood, too, when she rammed her forearm against Melanie's face.

She howled in pain, cursed even more and tried to bash Caitlyn against the head with the gun. Caitlyn dodged it and dropped her weight onto the woman, pinning her arms to the ground. That didn't stop Melanie from screaming and fighting, and just when Caitlyn wasn't sure how much longer she could hold her, she heard the movement behind her.

Since she hadn't been able to look back and see what was going on, Caitlyn didn't know if this was friend or foe approaching her. Worse, there was nothing she could do because if she let go of Melanie, she would pull the trigger.

The fear rose inside Caitlyn as the hurried footsteps got closer and closer, but she tried to steel herself for whatever might happen.

"It's all right," someone said.

Drury.

The relief nearly caused Caitlyn to go limp. Temporary relief, anyway. She still wasn't sure he was okay.

He wrenched the gun from Melanie's hands and moved Caitlyn off her so he could flip Melanie onto her stomach. He restrained her with some plastic cuffs that he took from his pocket.

Caitlyn pulled in her breath and held it. Until Drury finally turned and looked at her. He had some blood on his face. No doubt from the fist-fight with the hired gun, but he was all right.

"You shouldn't have done that," he said, his breath gusting. "She could have killed you."

"She didn't," Caitlyn managed to say, but she could see from the stark look in Drury's eyes that this had almost certainly triggered some flash-backs of Lily's death.

Even though Drury didn't exactly have a wel-coming expression, Caitlyn leaned in and kissed him. A very quick one because his attention went back to where she'd last seen Dade, Kara, Nicole and those other goons.

Caitlyn snapped in that direction, too, and she spotted Dade hurrying toward them. He had Ni-cole in his arms. Kara was right behind him, and she was still keeping watch all around them.

"What happened to the gunmen?" Caitlyn asked.

Kara shook her head. "All dead."

It was hard to feel any grief over the deaths of hired killers, but Caitlyn also knew that if they'd managed to keep at least one of them alive, then he could perhaps spill details they might not get from Melanie.

"You think this is over?" Melanie snarled when Drury hauled her to her feet. She looked back at Caitlyn, and the raw hatred was all over the woman's face. "It's not over. You'll never see your daughter again."

Chapter Twenty

"Hurry," Caitlyn insisted.

Though she really didn't have to remind Drury to do that. He already was in the "get there fast" mode and hadn't even waited for backup to arrive. Instead, Caitlyn and he had taken the car that Melanie and her thugs had used. It was a risk since there could be some kind of tracking device on the vehicle, but Drury weighed that risk against an even greater one.

Not getting to the baby before there was an attack at the ranch.

"Do you have a signal yet?" he asked, tipping his head to the cell phone she was holding.

Caitlyn shook her head. Cursed. It was frustrating, all right, but they'd be out of the dead zone soon, and she should be able to call the ranch. And Grayson. Drury had no idea what was going on with him, and it was entirely possible that Melanie had had another team of attackers go after the lawmen in the sheriff's office.

As Drury continued to do, Caitlyn glanced all around them. Watching for more of those hired guns. He was certain that Kara and Dade were doing the same thing. They'd taken the SUV so they could get Melanie to jail and Nicole to the hospital.

The surrogate was yet another concern.

Her injuries could be life threatening. Of course, Melanie was high on his list of worries, too, because she could have arranged for more gunmen to be positioned on the road. He didn't know how many hired killers that the million dollars of ransom money would buy, and Drury didn't want to find out.

"What do you think Melanie did to Jeremy?" Caitlyn asked.

Drury hadn't had time to give it much thought, but he didn't need a lot of thinking time to know that it probably wasn't something good. Melanie had been plenty riled over Jeremy's rejection and betrayal, and she'd no doubt set him up somehow to take the blame for all of this.

He took another turn onto a farm road, heading toward the ranch, but they were still a good ten minutes out. Drury figured it would seem more like an hour before they got there.

"Finally," Caitlyn said, looking at the phone

screen. Her hands were shaking when she pressed Grayson's number.

Drury hoped that his cousin would answer on the first ring. And he did.

"You two okay?" Grayson immediately asked.

"Yeah, but Melanie might have sent someone to attack—"

"I just got off the phone with Dade, and he told me. I've alerted the ranch hands, and Nate, Mason and our cousin Sawyer are heading down to the road now to make sure no one is there."

Caitlyn's breath rushed out from relief. They weren't out of the woods yet, but there was no way his cousins would let Melanie's thugs get close enough to do any real damage.

"I told Ronnie that we had Melanie in custody," Grayson went on, "and he's ready to spill all for a plea deal."

Drury had to shake his head. "If Ronnie was working for Melanie, why did she bring him at gunpoint to the jail?"

"Ronnie says that's the plan they worked out. That she'd pretend to turn him in, and that he'd take the fall in exchange for his kids getting a ton of money. He figures there won't be a payoff now that Melanie's being arrested."

No, there wouldn't be. In fact, Melanie's accounts would be frozen, and Caitlyn would get back any portion of the ransom money that Melanie hadn't spent on these attacks. Of course, that was probably the last thing on Caitlyn's mind right now. She just wanted to see her baby and make sure she was all right.

"Let me call you back after I've finished talking with the DA," Grayson continued. "Oh, and be careful when you make it to the ranch."

Drury would be, but he doubted he was going to be able to hold Caitlyn back. She had such a grip on his phone that she would probably have bruises. Bruises to go with the ones on her face.

It turned his stomach to see them. To know just how close he'd come to losing her.

"After this is done," he said, "I intend to chew you out for going after Melanie like that."

"You would have done the same thing if you'd been me."

He would have. "But I'm an FBI agent trained to do things like that." He paused, huffed. "That doesn't trump motherhood, though."

She made a sound of agreement. Followed by a helpless moan. "Please just hurry," Caitlyn repeated.

Drury did, taking the final turn. When the ranch finally came into view, he saw something that had him hitting the brakes.

There were men clustered around the cattle gate at the start of the ranch road, and someone was on the ground.

Hell.

Drury hoped he hadn't driven Caitlyn into the middle of another attack. Just in case, he turned off the headlights and eased closer. While he was trying to get a better look at what was going on, his phone buzzed, and he saw Mason's name on the screen.

"Is that Caitlyn and you in the car?" Mason growled.

Drury felt some of the tightness ease up in his chest. If Mason could call them, then he was okay. Well, maybe.

"Yes. What happened?" Drury asked.

"This dirthead we've got on the ground thought it would be a good idea to try to shoot something at the ranch. Trust me, he knows now it wasn't a good idea. We're about to haul him off to jail."

"Is Caroline okay?" Caitlyn asked.

"She's fine. Josh and Bree are with the nanny and her."

Josh, his other cousin, and Bree, who was Kade's wife and had once been in law enforcement. Caroline was in good hands. Better yet, she was safe.

Caitlyn's breath rushed out again. And the tears came. Tears of relief, no doubt. The happy tears would come once she had her baby in her arms.

"Was the hired gun alone?" Caitlyn asked.

"He was," Mason verified. "But we've got the

hands patrolling the area just in case. They found the clown's car just up the road, and there are no signs that anyone else was in it."

Maybe because Melanie had thought one fire-bomb shooter was enough. Or perhaps the woman had just wanted to save a little money.

"The gate and the fences are all armed, though," Mason went on. "So the alarm will sound if there are any stragglers who try to get onto the grounds. Someone's also monitoring the security cameras."

Good. It was a lot of security, but it had obviously worked since they'd caught this guy before he'd managed to do any damage.

He watched as Nate and Sawyer got the hired gun to his feet and started moving him toward a car that was nearby.

"Is it okay for me to drive Caitlyn to the guest-house?" Drury asked Mason.

Mason kept his glare on the man being arrested. "Yeah, because if this dirthead moves even an eyelash, he's going to pay and pay hard. It's too late to be testing my patience."

Drury wondered if it was ever a good time to test Mason's patience, but he didn't say that to his cousin. He drove onto the ranch.

"By the way," Mason said just as Drury was about to end the call. "Have you fixed things with Caitlyn yet?"

Since they were on speaker, Drury hesitated

before he said anything. "Fix things?" he settled for asking.

Mason cursed. "Have you told her you're in love with her? And no, the question isn't for me. It's because I know when I get back home, Abbie will ask me how the personal stuff worked out for you two."

Drury glanced at Caitlyn, who seemed a little shell-shocked. Maybe because of the whole ordeal she'd just been through. Maybe in part because of Mason's *you're in love with her* comment.

"I'll keep you posted," Drury answered, and he didn't bother to take out the sarcasm.

There was a ranch hand at the main entry gate, and he ushered Drury in, closing the gate behind them. Yet another security measure that Drury appreciated.

When Drury approached the guesthouse, he parked as close to the front porch as possible, and the moment he stopped, Caitlyn hurried out. He didn't try to stop her. No chance of doing that. So, he just raced in after her.

With all the chaos that'd gone on, being in the quiet room seemed a little surreal. The baby was asleep in her bassinet. Josh was sitting next to her, guarding her, and Bree was at the kitchen table quietly looking at the feed from the cameras.

"She's okay," Bree assured Caitlyn. Maybe because Bree was a mother herself, she no doubt figured Caitlyn would want to hear that right off.

"Thank you," Caitlyn said, and she repeated it several more times while she scooped up the baby. She pressed a flurry of kisses on her cheeks and held her close. Drury wondered if she'd ever let Caroline out of her sight again.

"She's a quiet baby," Josh added. "Unlike mine and most of the others on the ranch."

That was true. There were several contenders for the loudest Ryland kid, and Josh's was one of them.

"You think you two will be okay without us?" Bree asked. "Lynette had the twins, and I'd like to go to the hospital to see her. If Kade will let me off the grounds, that is."

Kade probably wouldn't allow that for a while, not until they were positive all was well.

"Are Lynette and the babies all right?" Caitlyn asked.

Bree nodded. "Gage sounded downright giddy when he called and said that the C-section went well. The boys are little, only four pounds each, but otherwise healthy. I could hear them crying in the background."

Great. More criers. More kids. But Drury found himself smiling at that thought. He'd never wanted to live on a quiet ranch anyway, and there was something comforting about knowing there'd be another generation of Rylands to run the ranch. Some of them might even follow in their footsteps and become cops.

"We'll be fine here," Drury assured Bree. Then he looked at Josh. "You can head home, too. The thug that Mason and the others caught is on his way to jail. Melanie, too." In fact, she was probably already there.

Caitlyn and Drury thanked them both again. Josh and Bree gathered up their things, both of them kissing the baby before they headed out. Drury locked the door behind them and armed the security system.

"It's just a precaution," Drury said when he saw the renewed concern in Caitlyn's eyes.

"Good. I don't want to take any more chances."

That sounded a little unnerving, as if she weren't just talking about security now. Maybe she wasn't ready or willing to take a chance on, well, him.

He eased down next to her on the sofa and was prepared to tell her how sorry he was that all of this had happened. But he didn't get a chance. That's because Caitlyn leaned over and kissed him. It wasn't a peck, either. This was an honest-to-goodness kiss, not of relief, either. This felt more like foreplay.

"The adrenaline," he said, ready to offer an excuse so she'd have an out. If she wanted an out, that is.

Apparently she didn't.

"I didn't kiss you because of the adrenaline," she insisted. "Or because we were nearly just killed." She paused. "Okay, maybe it did have a little to do with nearly dying, but things got crystal clear for me tonight when I thought I'd lost you."

Drury had experienced some of that clarity himself. "Yes," he settled for saying.

She stared at him, maybe waiting for more, and since Drury wasn't sure what more to say, he just kissed her right back. At first he thought she might be disappointed that they hadn't continued what could be the start of a promising conversation, but she moved right into the kiss. As much as she could anyway, considering that she still had the baby in her arms.

"You're very good at that," she said with her mouth still against his.

"I think it's just because we're good at it together."

Caitlyn eased back, met his gaze, and again she seemed to be waiting for him to say something important. Something that didn't have anything to do with what had just happened.

Drury finally managed to gather some words

that he hoped made sense. "I realized tonight that life's short. And there are no certainties."

She frowned but nodded. "You're talking about Lily now."

It was Drury's turn to frown. "No." And he wasn't. "I was talking about us." He had to stop and try to figure out how to say this. "I don't want you to leave. I want Caroline and you in my life."

At least she didn't frown, but Caitlyn did continue to stare at him. That wasn't the response he wanted, so Drury kissed her again, and he kept on kissing her until they were both breathless.

When they finally broke for air, she looked down at the baby. "She'll always be Grant's biological daughter."

He lifted his shoulder. In the grand scheme of things, DNA didn't seem important. "She'll always be *your* daughter. And I get what you're saying. Or maybe it's what you're asking. Can I accept her? Can I accept any of this?"

Caitlyn nodded.

Drury nodded, too. He could definitely accept it if Caitlyn was willing to stay and give them a chance. However, he didn't have time to spell that all out for her because his phone buzzed, and he saw Grayson's name on the screen.

Hell, he hoped something bad hadn't happened.

"Put it on speaker," Caitlyn insisted, and she eased the baby back into the bassinet as if preparing herself for one more round of the nightmare that they'd thought was finished.

"Are you two all right?" Grayson asked the moment Drury answered.

"Yes," they both answered cautiously. It was Drury who continued. "Did something else go wrong?"

"Not here. Why? Did something go wrong there?"

"No." Drury looked at Caitlyn. But everything wasn't all right just yet. He still needed to tell her so many things. First, though, he had to get through this call with Grayson.

"Dade just called me from the hospital," Grayson explained a moment later. "Nicole is being examined now, but the doctor doesn't think her injuries are life threatening."

Drury could see the relief in Caitlyn's eyes. Could hear it also in the slow breath she released.

"I've already got the approval from the DA for a plea deal with Ronnie," Grayson went on. "Don't worry, he'll still get plenty of jail time, but in exchange for testifying against Melanie, he won't be charged with murder."

"Murder?" Drury and Caitlyn asked at the same time.

Grayson paused. "Jeremy's dead. I've only spent about ten minutes with Ronnie, but according to him, Melanie set it up to look like a suicide, and in the note he confessed to killing Caitlyn and you. Grant, too."

"Melanie said Jeremy did murder Grant," Drury explained. "No proof, of course. And at this point we might never know for sure since Jeremy's dead."

"You're right. And I don't believe everything in this fake note. In it, he claims that Helen is responsible for stealing the embryo from Conceptions."

"But she didn't?" Caitlyn said under her breath.

"No, it was all Melanie, and Ronnie even has some proof. Guess he didn't completely trust his boss because he recorded some conversations that he says will prove Melanie was scheming to get both the baby and the ransom money. The recordings won't be admissible in court, but Ronnie can testify against everything on them."

That would tie everything up. Well, except for Helen and Jeremy. Jeremy was dead, and Helen had lost another son. Even though they obviously weren't close as most mothers and sons, Drury figured she'd still feel that loss. That didn't mean he had much sympathy for the woman.

"Helen's not getting Caroline," Drury insisted.

Caitlyn had a new look in her eyes now, one of thanks for backing her up. Drury intended much more than playing backup for her, though.

"Can't see how Helen would have a claim," Grayson agreed. "Caitlyn doesn't have as much as a parking ticket, and none of what happened was her fault. When I tell Helen about Jeremy, I'll remind her that if she ever wants to see her grand-daughter, then she'd better try to mend fences with Caitlyn."

That might work, and if it didn't, Drury would have a chat with the woman. After everything that Caitlyn had been through, he didn't want her to have to deal with the likes of Helen.

"What about Nicole?" Caitlyn asked. "Other than being the surrogate, please tell me she didn't have any part in this nightmare."

"According to Ronnie she didn't. I asked. He said Nicole didn't have a clue what was going on, not even after Melanie decided to have her kid-napped and held hostage. I'm sure Ronnie will give us a lot more info on how that all went down."

Yes, it sounded that way. Which was a good thing considering Melanie's other hired guns were all dead and wouldn't be able to spill their guts the way Ronnie was doing.

"Guess you heard that Lynette had the babies?" Grayson continued a moment later.

"Bree told us," Drury answered. "She said Ly-nette and the babies were doing okay."

"They are. Gage maybe not so much. He's crazy happy, but I figure it'll soon sink in that he's not going to get much sleep for the next few years what with twin boys in the house. By the way, has anyone mentioned that the females are seriously outnumbered on the ranch?"

Drury was instantly suspicious. "Mason said something about that. Any reason you're bringing it up?"

"You're a smart man. You figure it out." And with that, Grayson hung up.

This was Grayson's attempt at matchmaking, and he sucked at it. He was about as subtle as all the Ryland kids piled into the same room.

He put away his phone, checked the baby to make sure she was okay. She was. Then he looked at Caitlyn.

Not okay.

She was frowning again, and after all the good news they'd just gotten, that expression shouldn't be on her face. Especially since the frown was paired with a determined look in her eyes.

"I'm in love with you," she said as if it were a declaration of war. "I know that's probably not what you want to hear, but I can't undo my feelings for you. That doesn't mean you owe me anything—"

Drury stopped her with a kiss, one of those long ones that did more than rob them of their breaths. The heat slid right through him.

"I don't want you to undo your feelings for me," he assured her. "And having you say you love me is exactly what I want to hear."

She blinked. "Really?"

"Oh, yeah. Because I'm in love with you, too."

Finally, that got the frown off her face and erased the doubt in her eyes. She smiled. Kissed him until he was certain if they kept kissing, it was going to lead them straight to the bed.

Or the sofa.

Smiling in between the kisses, Caitlyn eased him back until his head was against the sofa's armrest. She didn't stop there, thank goodness. She slid her body on top of his.

"So, where do we go from here?" Caitlyn asked, glancing down at their new position.

Drury didn't think she was just talking about sex, and neither was he. "Everywhere. I love you, Caitlyn."

"And I love you," she repeated, pulling him to her.

* * * * *

Don't miss the final book in USA TODAY *bestselling author Delores Fossen's*
THE LAWMEN OF SILVER CREEK RANCH
miniseries when LUCAS goes on sale next month.

You'll find it wherever Harlequin Intrigue books are sold!

Get 2 Free Books,
Plus 2 Free Gifts—

just for trying the
Reader Service!

Get 2 Free Books,
Plus 2 Free Gifts—
just for trying the Reader Service!

HARLEQUIN® *Romance*

HRLP17R

Get 2 Free Books,
Plus 2 Free Gifts—
just for trying the Reader Service!

HARLEQUIN *super romance*

HOMETOWN HEARTS ♥

YES! Please send me **The Hometown Hearts Collection** in Larger Print. This collection begins with 3 FREE books and 2 FREE gifts in the first shipment. Along with my 3 free books, I'll also get the next 4 books from the Hometown Hearts Collection, in LARGER PRINT, which I may either return and owe nothing, or keep for the low price of $4.99 U.S./ $5.89 CDN each plus $2.99 for shipping and handling per shipment*. If I decide to continue, about once a month for 8 months I will get 6 or 7 more books, but will only need to pay for 4. That means 2 or 3 books in every shipment will be FREE! If I decide to keep the entire collection, I'll have paid for only 32 books because 19 books are FREE! I understand that accepting the 3 free books and gifts places me under no obligation to buy anything. I can always return a shipment and cancel at any time. My free books and gifts are mine to keep no matter what I decide.

262 HCN 3432 462 HCN 3432

Name	(PLEASE PRINT)	
Address		Apt. #
City	State/Prov.	Zip/Postal Code

Signature (if under 18, a parent or guardian must sign)

Mail to the **Reader Service:**
IN U.S.A.: P.O. Box 1867, Buffalo, NY. 14240-1867
IN CANADA: P.O. Box 609, Fort Erie, Ontario L2A 5X3

* Terms and prices subject to change without notice. Prices do not include applicable taxes. Sales tax applicable in NY. Canadian residents will be charged applicable taxes. This offer is limited to one order per household. All orders subject to approval. Credit or debit balances in a customer's account(s) may be offset by any other outstanding balance owed by or to the customer. Please allow 4 to 6 weeks for delivery. Offer available while quantities last. Offer not available to Quebec residents.